"Has it lingered in your mind? It has mine."

"In a way," Cari said, twisting her necklace charm. Dec noticed it had two initials. DJ.

No, it couldn't be. She wouldn't have waited so long to tell him.

"What are you saying?" he asked.

"There's no way to say this nicely. I had a baby nine months ago. A boy." She couldn't seem to stop talking now. "I should have called you but at first I didn't believe I was pregnant and then your company was planning a hostile takeover of mine and..."

He heard nothing. "I have a son?"

Dec had to figure out what to do with this information. A child. His child.

His heart skipped a beat and his stomach clenched. This changed everything.

* * *

His Instant Heir is part of the Baby Business series: One hostile takeover, two feuding families, three special babies

Dear Reader,

I'm sure you've noticed our exciting new look! Harlequin Desire novels will now feature a brand-new cover design, one that perfectly captures the dramatic and sensual stories you love.

Nothing else about the Harlequin Desire books has changed. Inside our pages, you'll still find wealthy alpha heroes caught in unforgettable stories of scandal, secrets and seduction.

Don't miss any of this month's sizzling reads....

CANYON by Brenda Jackson
(The Westmorelands)

DEEP IN A TEXAN'S HEART by Sara Orwig
(Texas Cattleman's Club)

THE BABY DEAL by Kat Cantrell
(Billionaires & Babies)

WRONG MAN, RIGHT KISS by Red Garnier

HIS INSTANT HEIR by Katherine Garbera
(Baby Business)

HIS BY DESIGN by Dani Wade

I hope you're as pleased with our new look as we are. Drop by www.Harlequin.com or use the hash tag #harlequindesire on Twitter to let us know what you think.

Stacy Boyd

Senior Editor

Harlequin Desire

KATHERINE GARBERA

—

HIS INSTANT HEIR

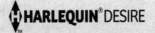

H HARLEQUIN® DESIRE

This book is dedicated to Rob Elser,
who makes me remember that it's not that hard to live happily-ever-after
if you have someone next to you who wants to be there.

Acknowledgments:

It's impossible for me to write a book about gaming and not thank my incredibly
wonderful husband, Rob. He is responsible for me having a gamer account on
Xbox 360 (RomWriter) and for my new skills as a first-person shooter—
I'm a pretty good shot, BTW.

I'd also like to thank the very talented Nancy Robards Thompson, who introduced
me to *Save the Cat!* and helped me jump-start my plotting when I was stuck.

Lastly, thanks to Charles for his insight and notes
on the early stages—they were invaluable
as always.

ISBN-13: 978-0-373-73262-3

HIS INSTANT HEIR

Copyright © 2013 by Katherine Garbera

PLEASE RECYCLE THIS PRODUCT IS RECYCLABLE

Recycling programs
for this product may
not exist in your area.

Printed in U.S.A.

H HARLEQUIN®
www.Harlequin.com

Books by Katherine Garbera

Harlequin Desire

¤*Reunited...With Child* #2079
The Rebel Tycoon Returns #2102
§§*Ready for Her Close-up* #2160
§§*A Case of Kiss and Tell* #2177
§§*Calling All the Shots* #2196
+*His Instant Heir* #2249

Silhouette Desire

¶*In Bed with Beauty* #1535
¶*Cinderella's Christmas Affair* #1546
¶*Let It Ride* #1558
Sin City Wedding #1567
¶*Mistress Minded* #1587
¶*Rock Me All Night* #1672
∆*His Wedding-Night Wager* #1708
∆*Her High-Stakes Affair* #1714
∆*Their Million-Dollar Night* #1720
The Once-A-Mistress Wife #1749
**Make-Believe Mistress* #1798
**Six-Month Mistress* #1802
**High-Society Mistress* #1808
Ω*The Greek Tycoon's Secret Heir* #1845
Ω*The Wealthy Frenchman's Proposition* #1851

Ω*The Spanish Aristocrat's Woman* #1858
Baby Business #1888
§*The Moretti Heir* #1927
§*The Moretti Seduction* #1935
§*The Moretti Arrangement* #1943
Taming the Texas Tycoon #1952
★*Master of Fortune* #1999
★*Scandalizing the CEO* #2007
★*His Royal Prize* #2014
¤*Taming the VIP Playboy* #2068
¤*Seducing His Opposition* #2074

¶King of Hearts
∆What Happens in Vegas...
**The Mistresses
ΩSons of Privilege
§Moretti's Legacy
★The Devonshire Heirs
¤Miami Nights
§§Matchmakers, Inc.
+Baby Business

Other titles by this author available in ebook format.

KATHERINE GARBERA

is a *USA TODAY* bestselling author of more than forty books who has always believed in happy endings. She lives in England with her husband, children and their pampered pet, Godiva. Visit Katherine on the web at www.katherinegarbera.com, or catch up with her on Facebook and Twitter.

Dear Reader,

Have you ever acted impulsively and then had to live with the consequences? That's what happens to Cari Chandler when she gives in to lust. I'd have to say this has never happened to me, but to be honest I do tend to jump without thinking of how I'm going to land—a lot.

While I was writing this book I read an interesting theory that says we make all of our important decisions in moments of crisis. For Cari that's what happened. The lust and one-night stand were meant to be just for that one night, but when she gets pregnant she has a really important decision to make.

Should she tell the father? Should she tell her sisters that this little boy will be the grandson of their most hated rival? And on top of that, *Oh, my God, I'm pregnant* is going through her head. So she does what she can and keeps the father's identity a secret until his family completes a corporate buyout of her family's company and she has to face him again.

I hope you enjoy this story since it was a lot of fun for me to write.

Happy Reading!

Kathy ☺

One

Cari Chandler paused in the doorway of the conference room. On the far wall was a portrait of her grandfather looking very young and very determined. Since he'd never been a "happy" man, she hardly noticed that he wasn't smiling. He certainly wouldn't be convivial at this moment when the grandson of his most-hated enemy was in his stronghold.

Since the late '70s the Chandlers and the Montroses had been feuding and trying to cut each other out of the video-game market. Her grandfather had won that long-ago skirmish by making a deal with a Japanese company, cutting Thomas Montrose out, but none of that mattered today as the Montrose heirs and their Playtone Games had just delivered the feud-ending blow with their hostile takeover of Infinity Games. And leaving Cari and her sisters, Emma and Jessi, to pick up the wreckage and try to forge some sort of deal that would save their jobs and their legacy.

But Cari as COO was the one who'd been chosen to deal with Declan Montrose. It made sense, since operations were her area, but the secret she'd been harboring for too long suddenly felt like it had a choke hold on her, and she wished she'd confided in her sisters so that maybe she wouldn't have to deal with Dec today.

The conference table was long and made of dark wood, and the chairs positioned around it were leather. She focused on the details of the room instead of the man she saw standing by the window. He hadn't changed much in the eighteen months since she'd last seen him.

From the back she could see his reddish-brown hair was a little longer than it had been before, but was still thick and curly where it hit his collar. His shoulders were still as broad, tapering to a narrow waist and that whipcord-lean frame that she'd remembered pressed against her as he'd held her. A shiver of sensual awareness coursed through her.

Don't. Don't think of any of that, she warned herself. Focus on the takeover. One problem at a time.

"Dec." She called his name. Her voice sounded strong, which pleased her since inside she was quaking. "I didn't think I'd see you again."

"I'm sure it's a pleasant surprise," he said with a sardonic grin as he left the window and walked over to stand not more than six inches from her.

The familiar smell of his spicy, outdoorsy aftershave surrounded her, and she closed her eyes as she remembered how strongly the scent had lingered on his skin right at the base of his neck. Then she forced herself to get it together, crossing her arms over her chest and remembering he was here for business. The knock at the door provided her with the distraction she needed.

"Come in," she called.

Ally, her assistant, entered with two Infinity Games logo mugs, handing one to Dec and giving the other to Cari. Cari walked around to the head of the table, already feeling more in control now that Dec was on the other side of it from her. She was aware of Ally asking if Dec needed anything in his coffee and him answering he took it black, and then Ally was gone.

"Please sit down," she invited, gesturing to the chair across from hers.

"I don't remember you being so formal," he said as he pulled out a chair and took his seat.

She ignored that remark. Really, what could she say? From the moment she'd first seen him she'd been attracted to him. Even after she'd learned he was a Montrose and technically her family's enemy, she'd still wanted him.

"I assume you're here to talk about moving assets around in my company," she said.

He nodded. "I'll be spending the next six weeks doing an assessment of the assets in the company and on this campus here. I understand you have three different gaming divisions?"

Wow. She should have been prepared for it, but he'd just completely shut off his emotions and switched to business. She wanted to be able to do the same, but she'd never been that good at hiding what she felt. Cyborg, she'd heard him called. He lived up to that moniker today.

He looked over at her and she realized she was just staring at him. This wasn't going to work. She'd call Emma, her oldest sister and the chief executive officer of Infinity, as soon as he left and tell her that she or Jessi would have to work with Dec. Though to be fair, as chief marketing officer, Jessi wasn't really the one who should be handling Dec.

"Cari?"

"Sorry. Yes, they all report to me—online, console and mobile."

"I will need to set up meetings with everyone in the company. The way this will work is that each person will be assessed and rated, and then I will give a presentation to our combined board of directors with my recommendations."

"No problem. Emma mentioned you wanted to talk to the staff. Do you think you'll just be here one or two days a week?" she asked, mentally crossing her fingers.

"No. I want to set up an office so I can be here in the thick of things," he said, leaning forward. "Is that going to be a problem?"

"Not at all," she said with the only smile she could muster. She'd rather not see him ever again, but that wasn't going to happen and she was mature so she could deal with it. She knew her smile must have looked forced when he laughed.

"You were never good at hiding your feelings," he said.

She shook her head. Though his statement was true, it wasn't something that he could know from personal experience. They'd had a one-night stand, not a relationship. "Don't say it like that. You don't know me at all. We only had one date and one night together."

"I think I got a fairly good impression of you," he said.

"Really?" she asked. She told herself to let it go and just concentrate on the business end of things, but that was going to be impossible. "Then why'd you leave me alone in that hotel room?"

He leaned back in his chair and took a long swallow of his coffee before standing up to pace around the room to her side of the table. He leaned back against the table and stared down at her, and she was tempted to stand up so he wasn't towering over her. But she didn't want him to think he intimated her.

"I'm not really a man for attachments," he said at last. "And though you think I don't know you, Cari Chandler, I'd have to be a blind fool not to see that you care too much."

She wanted to deny it, but the truth was she was the bleeding heart of the Chandler family. She volunteered, donated time and money to charities and causes and she'd fallen for more than one sob story at work. Emma had been furious at first, until she realized it made their employees loyal because they felt that the executive management cared.

"I wasn't going to cling to you and profess undying love, Dec," she said. She barely knew him after one sex-filled night. She might have been interested in seeing him again and getting to know him better, but she'd learned all she needed to know when he'd left her. "It was only one night."

"It was a fabulous night, Cari," he said, putting his hand on the back of her chair and spinning her around to face him. "Maybe I should remind you of how good we are together."

She pushed the chair back, standing up. It was time for her to take control of this meeting. "Not necessary. While I remember the details of the night, it's really the morning after that stuck with me."

"That's why I left," he said in that wry way of his. "I'm not good at dealing with the aftermath."

"Aftermath?" she asked.

"You know, the emotional stuff women usually bring up," he said. "The clingy things."

She shook her head. It was clear that a one-night stand was all that Dec intended for her to be. With her secret looming in her mind, she knew she had to say something about their night together, but for now she wasn't going to. She would focus on the business and try to figure out a way to save her family's legacy from being dismantled and destroyed.

Though she had to admit hearing Dec talk made her sad because she wanted better for herself. She had wanted to hear him say he wished he hadn't left and that he'd thought of her every day... Probably what he would term emotionally clingy stuff.

"Disappointed?" he asked.

"I guess I know why an eligible billionaire like you is still single," she said, trying not to be disenchanted that he was exactly like she'd thought he was. She'd hoped she'd just caught him on a bad day.

"Maybe the right girl just hasn't tried hard enough to change me," he said with a cocky half grin.

"Oh, you don't seem like the sort of man who can be changed," she said.

"Touché. I'm happy with my life. But that doesn't mean I don't know how to appreciate a woman like you when our paths cross."

She wanted to stay angry with him, but he was honest and she couldn't fault him there. Even though she'd hoped for longer with Dec, she'd known from the moment they'd gone to dinner that all he wanted was an affair.

"I think I'd have more luck changing the direction of the Santa Ana winds," she said.

"Have dinner with me and we can find out," he said.

"Would you be willing to discuss Playtone Games being a silent partner in Infinity?"

He laughed. "Not happening."

"Then neither is dinner." No matter how much he cajoled she needed distance and a chance to really think before she just jumped back into something foolish with him.

"We have to work together, so I don't think us spending time together outside the office would be wise," she said at last. She used to be more impulsive, but wasn't anymore. Her one-night stand with this man had reminded her there were consequences for acting without thinking.

"The Cari I know doesn't make decisions with only her head."

"I've changed," she said bluntly. Maybe if she hadn't fallen for his smooth-talking ways and blunt sexuality... What?

"I like it," he said slickly.

Cari knew she had to face facts that the man she'd had a one-night stand with was back in town. And it was becoming abundantly clear that a corporate takeover was the least of her problems. She was going to have to tell him about her son...his son.

Their son.

And she had no idea how to do that.

Cari had changed. That was easy to see even for a guy who'd spent only one night in her company. Dec knew things between them had always seemed complicated. Never more so than now. Their families were hated enemies of each other and his cousin, Keller Montrose, the CEO of Playtone Games, wasn't going to be happy unless Infinity was completely broken apart so that nothing of Gregory Chandler's legacy remained.

And this pretty blonde woman standing before him was going to be nothing more than collateral damage.

Dec had never been able to see her as his hated enemy. From the first moment he'd laid eyes on her he'd wanted to know more about her—and not so he could figure out how to use that information to take over her company.

Being adopted, Dec never truly felt like a real Montrose and was always striving to prove he was as loyal as both Kell and their other cousin, Allan McKinney.

Being back in California, conveniently with Cari, seemed his chance to do his job and continue to prove his worth to the Montrose family, as well as hopefully reconnect with the woman he hadn't been able to forget. With her thick blond hair that fell in smooth waves past her shoulders and her pretty cornflower-blue eyes, she'd haunted him. He couldn't forget the way she'd looked up at him as he'd held her in his arms.

Now that he had the chance to get a proper look at her, he could see the year and a half they'd been apart had added a quiet confidence to her. He started at her tiny feet in those pretty brown two-inch heels and moved upward. Her ankles were still trim, but her calves seemed more muscular. The hem of her skirt kept him from seeing any more of her legs but her hips seemed fuller…more pronounced. Her waist was still impossibly small, he noted, as the button on her jacket flaunted. Her breasts—whoa, they were a lot larger. She'd been slim and small but she was much—

"Eyes up here, buddy," she said, pointing to her baby blues.

He shrugged and then smiled at her. "I can see that you have changed a lot in the past year. Your figure is much fuller than before, but I like that."

He walked toward her with a long, languid stride and she backed up until there was nowhere for her to go. She put her hand up to stop him, keeping him an arm's length away. He stood there, staring down into her eyes, and had to admit there was something different about her. It was in her eyes. She watched him more closely than she had before.

She looked tired and he thought, well, duh, Playtone had finally gotten the upper hand on Infinity Games and she was more than likely worried about her job.

He backed away from her. "Sorry. I didn't mean to come on too strong. I'm sure losing your company to us was a shock."

"That's a bit of an understatement."

He smiled at the way she said it. "I'm a little jet-lagged still."

"Jet-lagged? I wasn't aware that there was a time zone between the Infinity Games campus and the Playtone offices," she said.

She gave up nothing. And he wondered how he could have missed this side to Cari eighteen months ago. But then he'd been in full-on lust and it was safe to say his brain hadn't been controlling him.

"I've been in Australia for a little over a year managing our takeover of Kanga Games."

"You let them keep their corporate identity," she said.

"They didn't screw our grandfather over."

"My sisters and I didn't either. We've always dealt with you and your cousins fairly."

"I'm afraid that doesn't matter when it comes to revenge," he said.

"Surely profit matters."

"It does."

She nodded and moved back to her chair. He sat down and so did she. She steepled her fingers together and he noticed she wore a ring on her right hand now that she hadn't before. It was a platinum band of hearts with a row of diamonds in the center. It seemed the kind of ring a lover would have given her. Was she involved with someone now?

Maybe that was where her new confidence stemmed from. She had a lover now. Well, he could be happy for her. Even though he regretted that he might not ever get to kiss her again.

"When did you get back from Australia?" she asked as she toyed with the ring. Those little gestures seemed to indicate her nervousness, though the rest of her body language didn't support that.

"Saturday, but I'm still adjusting. And seeing you again surprised me," he admitted, reaching for his briefcase, which he'd stowed next to his chair, and putting it on the table. He had his computer and the files he'd already started studying on the takeover.

"How did it surprise you? I knew you'd be here this morning," she said. "Didn't you know it would be me?"

"Yes, Emma informed me via email," he said. He wasn't about to tell her that he'd never expected to react so strongly to her presence. Not now. He'd thought since they'd slept together all the chemistry would be gone... but he'd been wrong.

The mystery of her body had been revealed to him. There wasn't an inch of it he didn't remember, though he realized now, with the flesh-and-blood woman standing before him, that those memories were a pale imitation of the real thing.

He wanted a chance to explore all of her curves and, more than that, he thought, to finally unlock the secrets she kept hidden deep inside. If he were busy dissecting her, maybe he would stop trying to get introspective in his own life.

In fact, the more he thought about it the more that Cari seemed the perfect distraction for whatever malaise had been affecting him lately.

He needed a distraction, and voilà, the universe had provided the one woman he'd hadn't been able to forget. He thought of his time frame for the takeover—six weeks. Surely that was long enough to satisfy his curiosity about her. Though being in the middle of a hostile takeover wasn't going to make seduction easy. In fact, if he were smart he'd forget about her personally and concentrate on business. But this was Cari, the woman whose image had haunted him throughout the past eighteen months, and now he wanted a chance to find out why. Was it just that he'd only had one night with her? Was there more between them?

"Then what's the problem?" she said with a half smile. She leaned boldly forward.

"There isn't a problem."

She stood up and put her hands on her hips. The movement pulled her suit jacket tight across her full breasts. She was a little bit flirty, which he liked. But also he sensed that it was a little forced this time.

"Are you sure? Doesn't it bother you that our families have been feuding forever?"

He'd like to say yes, but he suspected the problem was with him. He'd been traveling almost nonstop since he'd last seen her and he was a bit lonely for home. Not

the Baglietto Bolaro yacht he kept at the yacht club in
Marina del Rey that he'd christened *Big Spender.* Certainly not the Beverly Hills mansion that he'd inherited from his parents. He'd never had a place that he'd
felt was home.

It had just started three months ago, that longing for
something permanent. And he knew he had to get over
it. It was out of character for him. Being adopted by the
Montrose family was great, but being used as a pawn in
his parents' messy divorce had taught him that he was
meant to be alone. Then, at twenty-five, he'd lost his
father in a freak skiing accident, and two years later his
mother's liver had finally given out from all the drinks
she'd used to medicate her life.

He shook himself out of his reverie to answer Cari's
question. Was he bothered by the feud? Truthfully, it
was something he'd grown up with, part of his family,
and he knew it couldn't be ignored. Instead, he told
Cari, "It should." Though he was going to be unbiased
in his reviews, he knew Kell intended to fire all three
of the Chandler women in revenge for what had been
done to their grandfather all those years ago.

Starting an affair with Cari now had stupid written
all over it. And he wasn't a stupid man. He'd have to
work hard to keep reminding himself of that, because
the way she was now smiling at him made him almost
believe that an affair would work.

"I want a chance to convince you that Infinity should
be kept in its entirety," she said.

He saw her sincerity. He groaned deep inside because
that one statement gave him the excuse he needed to ask
her out again. He could even tell himself it was purely
business reasons why he wanted to go out with her, and

maybe he'd be able to convince himself that it had nothing to do with wanting to kiss her again.

"Have dinner with me tonight," he said. If she were involved with another man, she'd say no. "You can tell me about how you've changed and I'll tell you all the reasons why I like it."

She blanched, bit her full lower lip and then looked away. "I'm not sure that's a good idea. The next few weeks are going to be very complicated."

Not exactly a no, he thought. He wasn't sure what that meant for the competition or for him. "They are, but I see no reason why we should deny that we are friendly. I'm not saying we'll go straight back to my place after dinner—"

"We won't. I'm a lot more cautious now," she said.

"See, that's something I want to know more about. And we're both going to be too busy at work. Besides, this isn't the place for anything personal." He wanted to know more about her. He didn't feel like he'd had enough time with her eighteen months ago. Now he had the time while he was assessing her company.

"I agree," she said with a cheeky smile that made him want to go over and kiss her.

"Great. What time shall I pick you up?"

"I was agreeing to your statement," she said.

But he noticed she didn't say no to dinner. Finally she sighed, pushed her chair back to the table and stared over at him, searching for something, he couldn't really say what. But then she seemed to reach a decision and nodded. "Tell me where and I'll meet you at seven. Meanwhile, I'll have Ally get an office set up for you, but until one can be made available, you can work out of this conference room."

He let her be in control for the moment and watched

her walk swiftly to the door, her hips swaying with each step. He followed a few steps behind. She'd clearly dismissed him, and for Dec, that wasn't acceptable.

No matter what she wanted to believe, he was in charge of this entire operation—the business one and the personal one. And she'd just dismissed him like a servant—something that wasn't acceptable to him at the best of times, much less when he was still jet-lagged.

She turned and gasped as she realized how close he was to her. Then she licked her lips and he saw her gather her composure around herself like a shield.

God, he'd never forgotten the taste of her or how her mouth felt under his, and in this moment he wanted nothing more than to taste her again. He'd never had a problem going after anything he wanted, and until she'd waltzed into the conference room looking calm, cool and confident, he hadn't realized exactly how much he wanted her.

"Was there anything else?" she asked.

"Just this," he said, lowering his head and taking the kiss he'd wanted since she'd walked into the conference room and made him regret leaving her all those months ago.

Two

Cari hadn't planned on Dec. Not at all. Not the way his lips moved over hers or the way he tasted so familiar to her. She'd missed this, she thought. Then chided herself. She hadn't missed anything. Dec had been nothing but a one-night stand. It didn't matter that she'd wanted him to be more. He'd only been interested in her because of this.

Sex.

She only wished she could be dispassionate in his arms, but she'd been alone, her feminine instincts directed toward mothering instead of being a woman. Dec was awakening something in her that she thought she'd lost. A wave of desire shot through her. Her blood felt like it was heavier in her veins and every nerve ending came awake.

She wrapped her arms around his shoulders, knowing this was the only embrace she could allow between them, so she was determined to enjoy every second of it. She tipped her head to the side, angling her mouth under his, and sucked his tongue. He groaned, and for the first time since she'd learned he was back in her life, she felt a measure of control.

But control was fleeting. When he put his hands on her hips and drew her in so that she felt his erection against her lower body, she felt her breasts respond.

Shocked and afraid he might notice, she lifted her head and looked up at him. His eyes were closed and there was a flush of desire on his skin.

He was a hard man, but his lips were always so soft on hers. She lifted her hand and rubbed her thumb over his lower lip. She paused a moment, hoping for something that would resolve the conflict inside her. But then his hands tightened on her hips and she knew this was only bringing more complications to the table.

She dropped her arms and pulled her blazer around her to ensure that he couldn't see the wetness that would be a sure giveaway that she had a baby.

She sighed. She wasn't ready for Dec to come back into her life. She'd just settled into her routine with her job and her son, and now Playtone Games and Dec were throwing her back into a tornado. She wanted to grab DJ and her staff and head for the cellar until this passed, but she knew she couldn't run away. She was the one in charge of everyday operations and the take-over meant she was the best person to advise Dec on her staff. It was up to her to somehow persuade Dec to keep as many employees as possible.

He laughed. "Was my kiss that bad?"

"That good," she said, opting for honesty. She'd always been a lousy liar. Something her sisters had twigged on to the first time she'd refused to name DJ's father. But it had been important to keep her secret from them given the bad blood between Dec's family and hers.

"Then why the sigh?" he asked, his fingers flexing and drawing her nearer to him.

She put her hand between them to preserve the distance and her illusion of control, because it was becoming startlingly obvious that she hadn't been in charge of anything from the moment she'd walked into this conference room. She stepped back and stumbled into the door.

He reached out to right her but she shook her head. "I can't do this, Dec. We need to talk and there are things—"

"I'm not doing this for revenge," he said.

"What?" she asked. She hadn't even considered that, but now that he'd mentioned it, wouldn't it be fitting for one of Thomas Montrose's grandsons to take sexual revenge on his sworn enemy's granddaughter?

"I just wanted you to know that what is between us has nothing to do with business or our families. This is you and me. Just us," he said.

"Ah, that's a nice thought," she said, thinking of her son and her sisters and the fact that no matter what he wanted to believe, they didn't live on an island. It would never be just them.

"It's my opinion. I'm not one to let my cousins dictate my personal life," he said, touching a strand of her hair, tucking it back behind her ear the way she normally wore it. "I had the impression that you were someone who made her own decisions, as well."

"Of course I am. Stop trying to shame me into—" She stopped. "What exactly is it that you want from me?"

She felt panicked and nervous, but not because of

him. It stemmed from herself and the fact that it would be easy to surrender and give him what he wanted. A casual affair. But that wasn't like her at all. Dec Montrose was danger, she thought. She had to remember that.

"I want a chance. I don't want you judging me based on my cousins or this takeover. That has nothing to do with what is between us. It didn't eighteen months ago and it still doesn't now," he said.

"I agreed to dinner," she said. She struggled to believe him. If she was a sap, she'd fall for his lines, but she wasn't. Was she?

She crossed her arms over her chest, not really caring that it was a defensive pose. She had to figure out how to manage Dec. But managing people wasn't always her best strength. She preferred to help people find their happiness. And Dec wanted two things that wouldn't leave her in a good place. He wanted her company and she was almost 100 percent certain once he knew about DJ he was going to want their son.

"I want more than dinner," he said.

"That was obvious," she said.

"I've never been subtle. Kell says with this mug I can't be," he said, gesturing to his face.

He wasn't classically handsome, but there was something about that strong determined jaw and those dark brown eyes that had made it hard for her to look away from him in the past, and now. "You use that to your advantage."

He shrugged. "I figured out early in life that I had to play to my strengths."

"Me, too," she said. "I was never going to be as strong as Emma or as rebellious as Jessi. I had to find my own way."

"You've done well from what I can see. Everyone I talked to about Infinity Games said you are the heart of the company."

She closed her eyes and wished her staff had said she was the ballbuster of the company. That would make it easier for her to deal with him. What could she say about that? She genuinely cared about her staff and had made it her purpose to make sure they all worked to their maximum. "You're the axman of Playtone Games."

"So I'm the Tin Man then and don't have a heart. Is that what you're saying?" he asked.

She caught her breath at the flash of pain in his eyes. Just as quickly it was gone, and back was the determined suitor. She still wasn't sure what he really wanted from her, but she was determined to know this man better. She had until dinner to figure out the best way to tell him about DJ. She had until tonight to figure out if there was a way to use him to save as many of her staff as she could. She had until tonight to find a way to handle everything he threw at her.

She had a bad feeling the latter was going to be much harder than any of the others.

Dec had always felt like he wasn't the same as everyone else. The adult in him knew it had everything to do with him being adopted. His mother had insisted he be treated like the other Montrose heirs, but inside Dec had always known he wasn't a true heir. And that had affected him.

Normally he didn't give a crap about that. He knew he'd been called a shark. Cold and heartless when it came to his approach to business. A man who coolly cut staff, sent them packing and didn't apologize for it. That was business. Usually the people who complained were the ones who didn't make the cut. But hearing Cari say he was heartless had given him pause.

"Tin Man, really?" he asked when he realized she wasn't going to respond to his comment.

Ah, hell, he thought, pushing his hands through his hair. "Well, Cari?"

"I didn't mean it that way," she said, but he noticed she bit her lower lip and didn't lower her arms. She in fact did mean it that way.

"I'm not here to hurt you or your company," he said. "In fact, as a shareholder I'd think you'd be happy about the takeover. Despite the enmity between our families, you are going to be a very rich woman when this is all over."

"Is money the most important thing to you, Tin Man?" she asked teasingly.

"I'm not a Tin Man."

"Sorry. I didn't say it to be rude," she said, then nibbled her bottom lip. "Well, maybe a little. I'm trying to figure you out."

It was there in her tone. She was hiding something, or maybe just hiding from him. Maybe she'd discovered that it was going to take more than one kiss to get over him. He sure as hell was winging from the embrace they'd just shared.

"Good luck with that," he said. "I have enough money to make life comfortable. It's a nice goal, though. Most people want more."

"That's true. Is that the reason most of our stockholders sold to you?"

"I didn't talk to them, so I can't say. But profit is why they invested in Infinity Games."

"I know. I just hate change."

Change didn't bother him and never really had. He

knew that life was one constant change. People who got comfortable in a situation found themselves… Well, like Cari right now. "I'm not heartless when it comes to staff. Is that your biggest concern?"

She shook her head and fiddled with the ring on her right hand. "Everything about you raises red flags, Dec. I wanted to be cool and sophisticated this morning. Instead I let you kiss my socks off and stumbled into a door."

"I like you the way you are," he said.

She gave him that half smile of hers that had originally drawn him across the Atlanta convention space to her booth. It was inviting and sweet and made a man want to do anything he could to keep her smiling.

"Good, because I'm too old to change."

He laughed. She was young enough and innocent, as well. Despite the fact that she was the spawn of his family's hated enemy, there was nothing malicious in Cari. "If you're old, I must seem ancient."

She tossed her hair and let her arms fall to her sides as she studied him. "Not old, but there is something ageless about you. I know you have work to do. My assistant will work for both of us…unless you have one who will be joining you here."

"No. I don't need an assistant and it's a cost savings to just utilize existing staff." He'd had an executive assistant a few years ago, but the man had become a liability when he'd started to get too chummy with the staff of the company they were dissolving. It hadn't been easy, but Dec had fired him. Not everyone was cut out to work in mergers and acquisitions. It required a person who could compartmentalize. And he was the king of that.

"Cost savings…is that how you always look at the business?" she asked.

Her tone said she didn't approve, but that didn't bother him at all. If she'd asked him something like this about their personal life, it might, but this was business. There was no place for emotions in the workplace. If something was losing money it had to be cut, and Infinity Games had made too many poor decisions. Perhaps leading with the heart instead of the wallet. It had left them vulnerable to a takeover and now Dec was here to clean it up. And he would.

"Yes, how else would I view it? It's all about the bottom line. That's how we were able to take over your company."

"I'm not a driven-by-the-bottom-line type of COO. I like to see my staff working and being productive."

"Maybe you should have been more focused on the bottom line," he suggested. She hadn't argued when he'd called her the heart of the company. In his experience, that meant the emotional one. He had the feeling that she had an open-door policy and never said no to any of her staff. He would love to be proved wrong, but he seldom was. That meant they were going to be at odds at work. Mentally, he shrugged.

What he wanted from Cari had nothing to do with business. He'd do his job and he intended to get to know her, as well. The two things were separate in his mind.

"I don't know. I mean of course I understand that profit has to be a driving force, but I always think about the people behind it. They need to feel safe to work at their best."

"It will be interesting working with you. I have the feeling I don't know you at all, Cari," he said.

"I'm sure you don't," she said. "Most men only see what they want to when it comes to women."

"Interesting thought," he said. "Whereas you see me as I really am?"

She flushed. "Sorry. I just hate the thought of you looking at a piece of paper and saying we need to cut head count when I know that head count means a person. A person who has a life that they are trying their best to balance."

"I'm not going to randomly reduce staff. We need to see where you are losing money, Cari. You have to know that your company isn't as profitable as it could be."

"Yes, I do. As you said, we'll have to work together to make it profitable again," she said. She reached for the door again and he had the feeling that she wanted to get away from him. Who could blame her? He'd given her two things to think about this morning.

"I'm sorry," he said quietly. Because he hadn't meant to reenter her life this way. Well, to be honest, he hadn't really meant to reenter it at all. She wasn't the kind of woman with whom he could have an affair. Even if there wasn't a decades-long feud between their families.

It wasn't just that she was the heart of the gaming company, she also was caring and compassionate and, he knew, worlds too soft for Beau and Helene Montrose's adopted son. The boy they'd fought over and eventually, when his mother had lost the argument, handed over to Thomas Montrose to be honed into a weapon to be used in this war against the Chandlers.

"This was never going to be easy," she said.

"How do you mean?"

"You left me without a backward glance, and probably thought our paths wouldn't cross again. Definitely like this. Now we have to work together and I'm going to try to save as much of my company as I can and you're going to—"

"Do what I do best."

"What's that?"

"Make this a profitable move for Playtone Games and somehow convince you that despite all of that I'm not really a Tin Man."

Cari entered her office and picked up the phone to call Emma. Then immediately put it down. The time to go running to her big sister had passed. She was a mom now, a decision maker. At work she didn't need Emma's advice and she'd made the difficult decision to stand on her own in her personal life, as well. She knew better than to backpedal now.

She couldn't help it, though. She felt scared and panicked at the thought of Dec just down the hall from her. And little DJ downstairs in the nursery. Two males who had the most influence in her life. One by her design, the other...by fate?

She shook her head. She wasn't going to figure this out right now and didn't want to try. She instant messaged her assistant.

Ally knocked on the door and popped her head around. "You wanted to see me?"

"Yes. I need you to draft a memo to the staff from me and my sisters letting them know that Playtone Games has taken over our company and we will be using the next six weeks to merge."

"Okay. Anything else?" Ally asked without hesitation or concern. Her assistant was thirty-two and had gotten married last summer, and Cari knew she'd just signed a mortgage on a new house. She had to be worried.

"Let them know that Dec Montrose is going to be

observing them for the next few weeks. Everyone who works to their full potential need not worry."

"Okay. I'll draft an email and send it to you for approval," Ally said.

"Thank you. Do you think we could get a temp in here to serve as my assistant?"

"Why?"

"Ally, I'm thinking of transferring you to finance. You have the skills to be in accounts receivable and that way you won't be attached to me," Cari said.

She wasn't sure how much any of the staff knew of the bad blood between her family and Dec's, but she didn't want to take any chances of Ally being a casualty of that old feud.

"That's not necessary."

"Being part of this office might be a liability," she warned.

"Like you said, if I do my job I'm fine. Besides, I'm not abandoning you," Ally said with a smile.

"Thanks. In that case, Dec and I will be sharing you as an assistant. Think of it as a dual-reporting relationship."

"Okay," Ally said.

As her assistant left, Cari leaned back in her chair and swiveled around to face the plate-glass windows that overlooked the Pacific Ocean. She took a deep breath, warned herself that if she didn't get her head together Dec was going to walk all over her. And she couldn't let that happen.

Her door opened loudly and she pivoted around to see Jessi standing there. She had thick black hair that she wore shoulder length with a thick fringe of bangs on her forehead. For shock value, she had a deep purple streak on the left side. On anyone else it might have looked frivolous but on Jessi it just added to her commanding presence.

"So, how's it look?" she asked, putting a Starbucks cup down in front of Cari before dropping down into one of her Louis XIV wing chairs. She wore a pair of skinny black trousers with a rhinestone top and an Armani tuxedo jacket. Cari loved her sister's bold style.

"Thanks for the skinny latte," she said, taking a sip.

"Figured you'd need it this morning, and with my cute little nephew you don't exactly have time to get one for yourself. So what'd he say?"

She didn't need to ask who she meant. She sighed. "Dec's here for blood. He pretty much said he's cutting the dead weight and going to find out where we are profitable."

Jessi propped one booted foot on her knee and leaned back, taking a sip of her own drink, which Cari knew was a mocha. Her sister was a rabid chocoholic. "Figured as much. Can you influence him at all? What do you think is the best approach?"

"Um…" That was a loaded question. Now that Dec was here and his family had the upper hand in business, Cari realized her sisters would be at a disadvantage once DJ's parentage became public knowledge.

"What? Did he threaten you?" Jessi said, jumping to her feet. "I've dealt with the Montrose clan before."

"You have?"

"Unfortunately. Allan McKinney was the best man at John and Patti McCoy's wedding."

Cari remembered Jessi being the maid of honor at her best friend Patti's wedding two years ago in Las Vegas. She recalled hearing nothing about Allan, however. "I didn't realize that," she said.

"Well, since we're feuding with his family I didn't

think I should talk about it. Besides Allan was a total jerk douche about a few things. I can see why there is bad blood between our families. Anyway, I spent the longest weekend of my life in Vegas thanks to him. If I need to go in there—"

"No. You don't need to do anything for me, Jess. Dec was fine," she said. Then she realized she needed to start laying the groundwork for Dec to be introduced as DJ's father. "In fact, we're having dinner tonight."

"You are? He must be nothing like Allan, who is an annoying jerk."

Cari laughed, and for the first time this morning she felt maybe it wasn't the end of the world. No matter what happened at Infinity Games, they'd be okay. They might be a bit worse for the wear, but her sisters and she would be fine.

Three

Dec rubbed the back of his neck as Ally escorted the lead programmer from the IOS team out of the conference room. He needed a long, stiff drink and an evening where he didn't have to think about staff reductions. It was clear to him that part of the problem with Infinity Games was the fact that Cari allowed her staff too much leeway. But that was neither here nor there. It was almost six and as he had a date for the first time in almost six months, he was leaving.

"Good evening, Mr. Montrose," the security guard said as he exited the elevator. The lobby of Infinity Games spoke of heritage. On the wall in large print was a list of accolades the company had garnered since its inception in the early '70s. Dec skimmed over the first one, which listed both Gregory Chandler and Thomas Montrose's names. The next accolade was a partnership with the Japanese video-game giants Mishukoshi, after which Thomas's name disappeared. And so began the family feud.

Dec looked at the guard. "Good evening. What was your name again?" he asked. He knew in takeovers it was important to have a face to go with every name on his list. Kell wanted this place gutted and soon there would be no need for two teams of security. And this man looked like a prime candidate for early retirement.

"Frank Jones," the older man said. His blue security uniform was neatly pressed, he presented himself in a well-groomed manner and despite his age, Frank was in good shape.

"Declan Montrose," he said, holding out his hand. The handshake was firm and strong. There might be some gray in his hair, but Frank's posture and attitude weren't as elderly as it had seemed from across the lobby.

"Who hired you?"

"Ms. Cari. She said we needed someone who took this job seriously and understood that security was the most important part of making a game," Frank said.

"And that convinced you to take the job?" Dec asked.

"That and her smile," Frank said.

"Her smile?"

"She has this way of making you feel like you're the only one for the job when she smiles at you. Makes me want to do my best," Frank said.

"She does have a way," Dec agreed. Suddenly he had an inkling of why Cari was so popular with her team. There was something to be said about being made to feel important. Obviously it was a skill that Cari had in spades.

His iPhone rang as soon as he was in his Maserati GranTurismo convertible. He glanced at the caller ID and wanted to toss the phone out of the car. He wasn't ready to download information to Kell, but as the man was his boss and not just his cousin, ignoring the call wasn't an option.

"Montrose here."

"Here, as well," Kell said. "Is it as bad as we feared?"

"Worse. The staff is really loyal. I think if we kick the Chandlers out we might have a mutiny. I've spent the better part of the day listening to how great they are."

"That doesn't concern me," Kell said. "We knew the takeover was going to be messy."

"And I'm mitigating the mess, but it's going to take some time."

Kell cursed under his breath. "You said six weeks."

"And that's still exactly how long I need. Calling and badgering me isn't going to speed it up."

"I know that. I was wondering how the Chandler girl was…Cari?"

She was nervous and sexy and sweet. But his cousin didn't need to know any of that. And if Dec had learned one thing from his socialite mother it was to keep some information to himself. "She's hiding something."

"What? There is no other investor in the wings," Kell said with surety.

"I'll find out what I can. But there is definitely something she's protecting. Maybe one of her sisters. From what I gather, the oldest one, Emma, is something of a barracuda. The staff spoke of her the way our team talks about you."

"I'll get in touch and see if I can find out what they are hiding. You keep working on Cari. I think that Allan's best friend is married to the middle Chandler girl's best friend."

"Why do you know this?" Dec asked. Kell just didn't

do personal stuff. If it didn't affect Playtone Games, usually Kell didn't bother with it.

"I had the misfortune to try to drink our cousin under the table last weekend and heard all about the girl."

So Allan knew the middle sister, and unless Dec was very much mistaken—and he was seldom wrong about anything—he himself was going to know the youngest sister very intimately. Again. And this time he was going to… What? He was the adopted son of the Montrose dynasty. He had been abandoned, adopted, pretty much left to his own devices again. He knew he wasn't a man for commitment. What could he do with Cari except have an elusive affair?

In fact the only thing he'd ever stuck with was his cousins and Playtone Games.

When he was in this twenties he'd tried to strike out on his own, but then Kell had called and the chance to be part of this new generation of game-making Montroses was too much of a lure. Dec still wanted to prove himself to a generation that was all but gone.

"You still there?" Kell asked.

"Yeah, but I've got to go. Dinner meeting tonight."

"With?" Kell asked. In the background Dec heard the sound of the evening financial news show that Kell watched religiously. He was a genius when it came to reading the market, which was in no small part the reason for their success.

Dec had always marveled that he and his cousins, Kell and Allan, each brought something unique to the table that no one else could. They made a very strong triumvirate, and though he knew he wasn't a blood Montrose, he was definitely a necessary part of Playtone Games.

"Cari," Dec said at last. "I'm having dinner with Cari."

"Good. I suspect that you will keep her off balance and maybe you'll be able to find out what she is hiding."

He intended to find out all of her secrets, he thought as he ended the call with his cousin. He wasn't as concerned that she was hiding something that would affect the takeover; frankly, at this point there was nothing else for the Chandlers to do to save Infinity Games.

He pulled into the parking lot at the Marina del Rey Yacht Club and parked his car. The Playtone offices were in Santa Monica just a few short miles from the Infinity Games offices. Something that Kell had done deliberately to make sure that every day when first old Gregory Chandler and now his heirs had gone to work they'd have to drive past the competition.

Tonight he wanted to see if there was anything real between him and Cari. There had to be a reason other than revenge that he was back in her life. He realized that he wanted to move Cari from competition to lover. His time in her bed had been too short and being this close to home always made him long for things he knew he didn't need and couldn't have. But for tonight he was planning to ignore all of that and just enjoy himself.

Cari stood in the foyer of her own house holding her son in one hand and her cell phone in the other. Canceling dinner wouldn't be construed as running away, she cajoled herself. But then DJ reached up and put his tiny hand on the collar of her shirt and made that sweet little sound. "Mamamama."

"Ugh," she said, tossing the phone on the hall table and walking back across the Spanish-tiled floor to the kitchen. She put DJ in his high chair and then leaned back against the cabinet. "What am I going to do?"

He just stared at her as she placed a teething biscuit on the tray in front of him. His eyes were brown. Not just any brown, but Dec brown. She knew that if she canceled this dinner, it would be solely due to cowardice. She knew that. Yet she was more afraid tonight than she had been this morning.

It had been one thing to see Dec in the office where she wore her business suit and had a certain air of authority, but this dinner—no matter how she tried to spin it—was more than business. He'd kissed her. And her body had almost betrayed her secret. She knew she had to tell him about DJ before he found out.

She touched her lips and remembered every sensation of his body pressed to hers. God, she thought, this was nuts. Just cancel and then run away.

Dec might be all into her at this moment, but their past told her that he moved on. His own words told her that he wasn't ready for commitment, and though a lot had changed in the eighteen months they'd been apart, she knew she couldn't just spring DJ on him. She owed herself, her son and even Dec more than that.

Some things once done couldn't be undone.

Her grandmother used to say that to her all the time when she'd been young and headstrong. Wanting to adopt a puppy or bring another cat or rabbit into the house. Grandma was always cautioning Cari to remember that when other lives were brought into the equation, it changed.

She gave herself one last look in the mirror. "Tell him tonight."

But the look in her own eyes and that feeling in her heart told her that telling him wasn't going to be easy.

But even though she wasn't a bossy woman like Emma or a badass rebel like Jessi, she'd never been a coward. And running away wasn't her style. Besides, she knew it was past time to tell Dec about his son. Until she did, he'd have one thing over her—guilt. She felt guilty about him not knowing about his son.

"I'm going," she said, smiling at DJ.

He clapped his hands and smiled back at her. She laughed at his toothless grin and drool-covered face. Truly he was the most adorable baby in the world. She scooped him up again and walked resolutely down the hall to her bedroom. She put his blanket in the middle of her bed and propped pillows around him to keep him in place.

He sat in the center, happily chewing on his biscuit while she puttered around getting ready for her date and awaiting Emma, who was going to babysit, along with her son, Sam.

The doorbell rang, and from the security monitor in her bedroom she saw not only Emma and Sam, but also Jessi. She wasn't ready for both of her sisters. Not tonight. She was so unsure, and hell, she had to admit, scared, that she was tempted to blurt out her secret to her big sister Emma. Then Emma would excuse her and—

Stop it.

She hated that she still sometimes wanted someone else to make decisions for her. She was a grown woman and a mom now. It didn't matter that it would be easier if she just gave up control of her life. She had to step up.

She pushed the intercom button. "Come in. I'm in the bedroom getting dressed."

She hurried into her closet and grabbed a retro-style cocktail dress that she'd gotten from ModCloth at a bargain. She didn't need to save money, but her mother had drilled into her that it was better in her pocket than in someone else's, and she'd always been frugal.

"Let's see what you are wearing," Jessi said as she led the way, ignoring DJ and coming into the closet to stand next to her. Her sister had an aversion for babies and was the first to admit she liked to keep her distance from children until they could walk, talk and order a drink.

She spun around so that Jess could see what she was wearing. The dress was slim-fitting, in a regal purple color that made her pale skin glow. It had a fitted bodice with thin spaghetti straps and a velvet ribbon that accentuated the slimness of her waist. She'd put on a strand of black pearls that their father had given their mother for a long-ago birthday and that Cari had inherited when her parents had died in a tragic boating accident, but she'd changed her mind at the last minute and now wore her usual charm necklace instead.

"Gorgeous, darling! Are you sure this is just a business dinner?" Jessi asked.

"Yes," she said, though the heat of her blush made her realize that she wasn't as confident in that answer as she should be. "What else could it be? He's a Montrose."

"Don't forget it," Jessi said as they both walked back into the bedroom.

Emma gave her the thumbs-up. "You look good," she said. "What are you not supposed to forget?"

"That Dec is essentially my enemy."

"Dec?"

"That's his name."

"His name is Declan, Cari. And you said it like…" Emma watched her shrewdly.

She didn't ask like what. Cari knew how she'd said his name. Like he was her salvation and her downfall.

And he was both. No matter how she tried to spin it.
No matter what she wanted to pretend. No matter that
he was a game changer and she had to decide how to
proceed.

So far she'd let him get the upper hand at the office,
and for her own sake and DJ's, she couldn't let that happen tonight. She had to be the one in control.

She glanced at both of her sisters as she sprayed perfume on her pulse points. They looked worried, and
she just smiled at them as she adjusted the high ponytail she'd put her hair up in and fingered the bangs on
her forehead.

Tonight she was going to be rebel, boss and angel
all rolled into one. Tonight Declan Montrose wouldn't
know what hit him. Tonight she would walk away vic-
torious.

Dec was waiting in the bar for her when she arrived at the Chart House restaurant in Marina del Rey.
He looked sexy and sophisticated dressed all in black.
Pants, tie, shirt and jacket. On anyone else it would have
looked like too much, but it suited him. He wasn't light-
hearted at all and this dark attire reflected that.

But it also made him look devastatingly handsome.
She noted that women sneaked covert looks at him as
they sipped their drinks. She sighed and wondered if
she was really up for this. Talking herself into being
brave had been a daily ritual since she'd realized she
was pregnant. She continued the practice now, put her
shoulders back and walked over to him.

He turned just as she approached. And she arched
one eyebrow at him in question.

"I saw you in the mirror," he explained, holding out
a drink. "I recall you were a gin-and-tonic girl."

"Still am," she said. "But since I need my head about me tonight, I'll settle for just the tonic."

He smiled. "I'll get you a different drink."

He turned back in a second handing her a highball glass with a twist of lime in it. She took a sip of the refreshing drink and decided to stop her worrying for tonight. Somehow she'd figure out how to tell him he had a child.

"How was it today?" she asked.

"I don't want to talk shop tonight. I want to catch up on you," he said. "We've got fifteen minutes until our table will be ready."

He led the way through the semicrowded bar to a small intimate booth in the far corner and gestured for her to sit. She slid onto the seat and took an inordinate amount of time to straighten her dress about her legs.

"I make you nervous," he said when she looked up.

"Yes. You did when we first met, as well," she admitted.

"Why? Is it because I'm a Montrose?"

She thought about it. But really she didn't need the time to consider his question. She'd already spent a lot of time dwelling on Dec Montrose. "No. It's something about you. You seem so confident and determined... makes a girl feel like she needs all of her wits about her."

"You don't seem to have a problem with me," he said.

"There are one or two ways to keep you off balance," she said. "But I can't always count on being able to kiss you."

His surprised laugh made her smile. The black clothing wasn't a front where he was concerned. Dec was serious most of the time. So when he did smile or laugh it felt like a sort of gift.

"I'm willing to let you try it."

"I bet. Tell me about Australia," she said.

He shook his head. "That's business."

"You haven't done anything but work for eighteen months?" she asked. "I don't believe that. You seem a bit different than before."

He shrugged and took a swallow of his scotch on the rocks. "It might be the fact that after ten years of hard work Playtone Games has finally met our goal."

"Taking over Infinity Games?"

"Yep," he said. "Guess you don't want to talk about that."

"No, I don't. I should have thought harder about going to bed with someone who has a decades-old feud with me."

"I'm not feuding with you," he said.

"Really?"

"Not anymore. I've won the battle. Now it's simply a matter of cleaning up the mess and moving on. No conflict of interest between us anymore."

But there was a big conflict of interest, and for the first time since she'd given birth to DJ she realized that her son could be the leverage she needed to make Dec do what she wanted him to. As soon as the thought entered her mind, she shuddered with repugnance and pushed it aside. She'd never use her own son as leverage. That was despicable.

As was not telling him. Though she believed her reasons were valid. He hardly seemed like the kind of man who'd want a family or a son. But she owed it to him to let him make that choice now that he was back in her life.

"So, there's something I should tell you," she said, not sure how exactly to begin this conversation.

"Is it a secret?"

"Sort of," she said.

"Kell did want me to find out what you are hiding," Dec said.

"What?" How did his cousin know she was hiding something? Did he know that she'd had a baby with Dec?

"I told him I thought the day had gone well, except I felt there was something you weren't telling me."

"Oh." So he assumed it was something to do with the takeover. Why wouldn't it be? They'd had a one-night stand, not an affair or a fling. He'd never guess what she'd been keeping from him because his mind wasn't going along that path.

"Well, he'll be disappointed. I'm not keeping any business secrets," she said.

"I think you are. The security guard said that the staff would do anything if you smiled at them."

She blushed. He had to have been talking to Frank, who was like a Dutch uncle to her. "Frank exaggerates. Besides, what would I get them to do?"

"Mutiny," he said.

"You're not the captain of a ship," she said.

"But I am. I'm the one who's going to steer them through the shark-infested waters—"

"I thought you were the shark."

"Only in your eyes," he said.

But he wasn't a shark in her eyes. She reached over and took his hand and squeezed it in hers. "The acquisition isn't going to be easy, but I don't blame you for anything you have to do."

"What do you blame me for?" he asked.

"Leaving me." The words just slipped out. But now that they had been spoken she realized they were the truth.

"I'm back now."

"Yes, you are. For some reason, I'm not sure why you are here with me. You already satisfied your curiosity with me, right?"

"I'm nowhere near satisfied with you, Cari. I want more and I intend to get it."

Four

Dec couldn't relax. All he could do was stare at Cari and wonder why he hadn't seen this side of her eighteen months ago. There was a confidence in her that had been lacking before. Now she flirted and leaned in to make a point, whereas before she'd let him take the lead and set the pace.

A part of him acknowledged that if she'd been like this in the hotel in Atlanta, he would have had a harder time leaving her.

"Why are you staring at me like that?" she asked.

"You're a beautiful woman…you must be used to men staring," he said.

She shook her head and looked away from him. "Not for a while. I've been busy."

"Busy at work?" he asked. Given the state that Infinity Games was in, he highly doubted it.

"Not just work. My life is crazy right now," she said.

"What do you do outside of work? Charities?" he asked. It was what his mother had busied her time with and what his grandmother had, as well.

"You sound a bit disdainful," she said. "There is nothing wrong with charity work."

"I know. But the women I knew who spent all their time volunteering rarely had time for their families."

"Ah, your mom?"

"Mother," he said. "She didn't like the informal *mom*."

"Really? I don't know much about your past," she said.

"Why would you?"

"We're mortal enemies. I have done a few Google searches on you," she said with a sparkle in her eye. She took another sip of the water she'd ordered with her main course and smiled over at him. "But the internet was mainly just business-related articles, so tell me more, Dec. Let me know what your kryptonite is."

"Who says I have a weakness?" he asked.

"Everyone has one."

"Even lovely blondes?"

"I don't know about any other blonde, but I definitely have a weakness."

"Do tell," he invited.

"Forget it, buddy. We were talking about you," she said.

Knowing about his past wouldn't reveal any weakness. To be fair, he doubted he had one. He knew that only if he genuinely cared for something or feared losing it would he then be vulnerable. Therefore, he had nothing to lose.

"Well, my mother and father were very busy people. Mother had her charity work and Father was consumed with trying to please Grandfather on his quest for revenge against your family."

"Surely they must have made time for you," she said.

He could see this turning into a sob story if he wasn't careful, and a woman as softhearted as Cari would eat it up. For a minute he weighed using her emotions to his advantage, but discarded that thought. He didn't need to cheat or prey on her senses to win. "There were the usual family functions. But we all lived our own lives. It worked for us. Sorry I sounded bitter about charities."

"It's okay. I do give money to charities—more than I care to say—but I don't volunteer. I spend most of my free time at home or shopping on the internet."

"Truly? I thought you were more social than that," he said.

"I used to be, but lately, what with you and your cousins gunning for our business, I've had other things to concentrate on."

"I can't regret it," he said.

"The chance to finally get one up on my grandfather?" she asked.

Sort of, but for him it was more about winning than settling an old debt. "Not at all. I'm glad we won so that I can spend more time with you."

She rolled her eyes. "It's not like you were knocking on my door and I sent you away. Why this sudden interest in me?"

It was the one question he didn't know how to answer. Not even to himself. He could only say after being so long in Australia and away from everything in the U.S., he'd had a chance to realize that he didn't necessarily have the same agenda as he used to.

"Maybe it's you."

"Yeah, right. Excuse me if I don't buy that."

"Well, tonight it is. I intended to pump you for business info—"

"Liar. You said yourself no business."

"I meant originally, smarty-pants. But once I saw you tonight, I forgot about everything but our night together and regretted I didn't stay."

She tucked a tendril of hair behind her ear, where it simply curled back against her cheek again. She nibbled her lower lip and then sighed. "It would have been complicated."

"Definitely, but I'm very good at managing complications."

"Oh, I think this one would have thrown even you," she said.

"Which one?" he asked. He had the feeling sometimes that they were having two different conversations. Part of that he could easily attribute to the fact that she was a woman and he a man and they just communicated differently. But there was more to it than that. Maybe her secrets?

"Us staying together after our night," she said. "Wasn't that what you were talking about?"

"Yes, but I meant because my cousins wouldn't understand it."

"Fraternizing with the enemy," she said on a wistful sigh. "That always sounds so romantic until you have to answer to your sisters."

He laughed. "Yes, it would have been difficult. Maybe I did us a favor by leaving."

"There is no us," she reminded him gently. "This is dinner, not a romantic date."

"That kiss in the conference room says otherwise."

"It had been a while since I'd kissed a guy. Don't feel special," she said.

Too late, he thought. He already did. There was something about her and her damned smile and her kisses that made him feel like the only man in her world.

"I'm wounded."

"Ha," she said, taking another sip of her wine. "It will take a lot more than one comment to put a dent in that ego."

"Why do you think so?"

"You walk into my office building and my conference room bold as brass as if nothing had happened between us. You tell me how you are going to dismantle my staff, kiss my socks off and then tell me we are having dinner together. How is that anything other than colossal ego?"

He took another swallow of wine to keep her from seeing his smile. His father had always said that Dec had more confidence than smarts. "I can't say it's all ego. You are here with me tonight after all."

"Touché."

"Makes it hard for a man not to feel special," he said. He wasn't looking for anything permanent with Cari. He knew himself well enough to know that now was the only place he was comfortable living—he didn't dwell on the past or long for the future.

After they finished their meal, Cari excused herself to go to the ladies' room and called her sister to check on DJ. She knew that Jessi would have been long gone and Emma would be alone with Sammy and DJ. It was eight-thirty, which was the time she usually settled onto the couch with her iPad and online shopped while her baby slept in her arms. But she knew Emma wasn't going to hold DJ all night the way she did.

"How's he doing?"

"He's restless. He just keeps calling for you," Emma said. "I thought this was his usual bedtime."

"I hold him until he goes to sleep," Cari said.

"That's what I was afraid of. Sam's piled up some pillows on the nursery floor and is reading to him."

"I didn't know he could read," she said. Her nephew was only three.

"Well, he mostly just flips the pages of the book and makes up a story to go with the pictures. Right now *Green Eggs and Ham* involves a badly cooked breakfast."

Cari laughed and felt a little pang as she missed her own little guy and her nephew. "Sammy is so good to him."

"He's wanted a little brother for a while now," Emma said. "This was supposed to be the year for that."

"I'm sorry," Cari said. No one had expected Helio to die so young. His death had been a shock to everyone. And Emma had retreated into full corporate-executive mode. To be honest, most of the time the only one who saw the human side of her sister was Sam.

"It's okay. How's dinner? Did he let anything slip?"

"Dinner is fine. We're going to have a nightcap at the marina. Will you be okay to stay?"

"Yes. As a matter of fact, I think I'll take DJ to my place. Maybe the car drive will put him to sleep. You can either swing by and get him in the morning or I will bring him to the nursery at Infinity Games."

"Okay. I'll miss him tonight."

"You'll be fine. Concentrate on getting some answers from Dec about what he plans to do next."

"I will do my best," she said. "I might stop by to-night."

"Whatever you decide. Take care."

"You, too," she said. After disconnecting the call, she touched up her lipstick and fixed her hair before heading back to the table.

She noticed that Dec was on the phone as she approached and hesitated, but then remembered what Emma had said. She needed to find out what he was doing with the company. But to be honest, her heart wasn't in it. He said goodbye as she approached so she didn't get any information.

"Ready to go?" he asked.

She nodded as he got to his feet. He put his hand on the small of her back and guided her through the tables toward the front of the restaurant. She could obviously have walked through the place without his hand on her, but a part of her liked it. Liked the heat from his body that seeped through the fabric of her dress. Liked the sprawl of his fingers over her back. Liked…well, just liked the feel of his hands on her.

She shivered as he rubbed his forefinger back and forth over the zipper that went down the center of her back.

"Chilly?"

She shook her head. Then realized she should have said yes.

"I've missed touching you, Cari," he said, leaning close so that his words carried no further than her ears.

She'd missed it, too. She stopped walking and stepped away from his touch. "You didn't have to."

"I've apologized."

"I know, but that doesn't give you a clean slate. I should just go."

"I thought you wanted to talk," he said.

"I do. But I can't if you're going to touch me."

"I was being polite," he said.

She knew she was overreacting and it wasn't totally his fault. It had been too long since a man had touched her and she'd been hungry for it. She wasn't sure how much was her hormones and how much could be attributed to Dec.

"I know."

He gave his claim tag to the valet. "Is it still okay to take my car to the marina and come back for yours?"

"Yes," she said. She hoped while they were having a drink she'd be able to tell him about DJ. But she still wasn't sure how to say it. Also, a part of her didn't want to tell him. She still wasn't sure he was ready to be a father.

"Here's my car."

"A Maserati?"

"Yes, I like my cars fast and sexy."

"Why am I not surprised?" she asked. "Have you ever thought about what you'll do when you have a family?"

"I'm not planning on one," he said. As he glanced around and she met his calm brown gaze, she realized that he spoke the truth. She'd hoped to learn more about him as a man and all she'd learned was that his mom was a volunteer who hadn't made much time for him. Maybe that was why he didn't want a family.

"Oh," she said, knowing she sounded a little unsure. But really, what else could she say?

"I'm too much of a loner."

Well, there you go, she thought as she climbed into the car. What was she going to do now? No matter what he wanted or even what she desired, he had a son and she was the mother of that child. Whether he was ready to be a father or not. She owed it to him to let him know.

It was just that her fantasy of him suddenly falling

to his knees and making declarations of love for her and DJ were gone. She realized that this was real life, not some fantasy world where everything was going to work out simply because she dreamed it.

"You okay?" he asked.

"Yes," she said. The miles to the marina flew by and Cari leaned her head back against the seat as the bluesy beat of Stevie Ray Vaughan flowed through the car. Stevie sang of heartbreak, and even though Cari knew she didn't love Dec she couldn't help but feel like she was a little heartbroken, too. It was the first time she realized that dreams could be broken as easily as a heart.

Dec felt the mood change as soon as they got to the marina. He was a member here because he lived on a yacht that was moored here. He'd learned a long time ago that he didn't want a big house, but he suspected that was his way of keeping himself different from his parents. He liked to pretend that all the stuff he could buy meant nothing to him. He doubted that Cari would be agreeable to a drink on his yacht, the *Big Spender*. His cousin Allan had named it for him—a tongue-in-cheek reference to the fact that he liked expensive toys.

He led the way through the member's-only club to a table set on the balcony far away from the other diners. It was quiet this time of night. He signaled the waiter and when he arrived Cari ordered a decaf coffee and Dec did the same.

"I seem to have said something that upset you," he said.

"I have something to tell you," she said.

"Go ahead," he invited.

"Um…it's not as easy as I imagined it to be," she said.

Now she was starting to worry him. What could she possibly have to say to him that was so difficult?

"Are you married?" he asked.

"No. I wouldn't have come to dinner with you if I were involved with another man," she said. "Commitment means something to me."

"It means something to me, as well," he said. "That's why I avoid it."

"Really? Did something bad happen to you in the past?"

"Yes."

"Tell me about it," she said.

Their coffee was delivered and the waiter left. But he didn't start talking. He didn't like to think of his past. Didn't like to discuss the fact that he was an orphan and his adoptive parents had been in a facade of a marriage. He was just the final piece in their perfect little image of a family. But none of it had been real.

"I'm not interested in the past," he said at last.

"But without the past we have no way of measuring where we are going."

"I'm more of a live-in-the-now man."

"But you have to plan for the future," she said. "Just having business goals would necessitate that."

He shrugged. "I'm driven at work. But it's more because I don't like to fail."

She shook her head. "I don't know what else to say. Or really how to say this. Our one-night stand…"

"Yes? Has it lingered in your mind? I know it has mine."

"In a way," she said, twisting the charm on her necklace with her fingers and then patting it down.

He glanced at the piece of jewelry, for the first time

noticing that it was a charm with a small head on it and two initials. DJ.

DJ?

He was starting to put things together but what he was coming up with made no sense. Whatever it was she was trying so hard not to say to him…it couldn't be what was flirting around in the back of his mind.

She wouldn't have waited so long to get in touch with him. He had to believe that.

"What are you trying to tell me?"

She took another sip of her coffee and then put both hands on the table and leaned over toward him. Even in the dim lighting he could see the tension in her body and the nervousness in her eyes. He calmed himself the way he did when he had to fire someone. He pushed down all the emotions that had been swirling around him all night—even the lust that he'd hoped would lead to more than just a kiss.

"It might sound… That is to say after you left— Dammit, there is no way to say this nicely. I was pregnant, Dec. I had a baby nine months ago. A little boy," she said. Now that she'd started talking she couldn't seem to stop. "I know I should have called you or gotten in touch but at first I didn't—couldn't believe I was pregnant and then…well, your company was planning a hostile takeover of mine and…"

"I have a son?"

"Yes. He's nine months old," she said. She fumbled for her handbag and pulled out her cell phone.

He ignored her as the thoughts circled his mind. He never planned to have a kid because he didn't know how to be a father or really what it meant to be part of a family, and he knew from his own upbringing that a bad parent could be worse than no parent at all.

She was saying something else to him but he couldn't hear her words. All he knew was that the plans he'd made for his life had just disintegrated. He had to figure out what to do with this. A child. His child.

She handed him her phone. He glanced down at the screen and saw his son for the first time. His eyes were the same deep brown as Dec's were. His smile was small and toothless and his eyes wide. It was easy to see the baby was happy. And Dec felt his heart skip a beat and his stomach clench. This changed everything. It added a complication that even Dec couldn't navigate easily.

He stood up, knocking his chair over as he turned to face the glass and saw a reflection of himself. He'd never belonged to anyone, not really, and now Cari had told him he had a son. The first blood relative he'd ever known of.

"I have a son?"

Five

Cari knew she could have handled the announcement a little better, but at least it was out there, and a part of her felt relieved. She'd always told herself Dec had made his choice when he'd left and she'd made the best decision for herself—to have her son on her own. She'd felt bad about keeping DJ a secret from him, but she'd had no other choice.

Dec was quiet and those warm brown eyes of his were cold and hard. She knew she'd given him a shock and she wanted to just finish the conversation and get out of the marina bar. She'd never felt this unsure in her life. Except maybe that moment when she'd held her son in her arms for the first time and realized that she wanted to give him the world but had no idea how to take care of him.

"Given that you said you don't really want a family—"

He spoke without moving his eyes from the picture on her cell phone. "That was before I knew I had a son. He has my eyes." There was a sense of awe and maybe a little nervousness in his voice. She'd never seen him like this before. This had shaken him.

Finally he put her cell phone back on the table and glared over at her. Aside from the occasional smile, this was the first real emotion she'd seen from him. He looked angry and, if she was being totally honest, scared. She had had months to get used to the fact that she was going to have a baby. And he'd grown inside of her, giving her a chance to adjust to the fact that he was real.

She felt a little guilty at how she'd sprung the announcement on Dec. He seemed shell-shocked. When he sat down again she reached for his hand, but he drew it away from her and stared stonily at her.

"I know he has your eyes," she said at last. "Listen, we have a lot to talk about," she added, taking control of the situation.

Once again she pretended she knew what she was doing, as she had every day since her son was born. It was important that Dec not doubt her. It was important that he thought she knew what she was doing. Because if she let her confidence slip for a second she knew he'd try to take over. "I didn't try to contact you because there were all those months before I knew I was pregnant when you didn't get in touch. It kind of seemed like you'd moved on and I had to move on, too."

"You still should have—"

"What? Even today you're not exactly warm and welcoming unless you count that kiss in the boardroom and frankly, I can't. I don't have the luxury of waiting around to see if you have changed. I'm a mother now, Dec. I have someone else counting on me."

He looked at her as if he'd never seen her before, and she just stared back at him. She'd spoken the truth. No one, not even this man, was going to protect her son the way she did. And she kept that in mind as she sat across from him now.

He sighed and tunneled his fingers through his thick hair, leaving it rumpled. His hands shook when he reached for his coffee and she wondered what was going on in his mind. But then she'd never really been good at guessing his motivations.

"Okay, let's stop the blame game," he said. "I behaved… Well, it doesn't matter. I used a condom."

She'd agonized over that moment a million times. He had used protection, and though she hadn't been on the pill, she'd thought they were safe. It was only when she'd started feeling queasy and then throwing up six weeks later that she'd thought… Well, she'd denied it could be anything but an upset stomach from spending too many months on the road at conferences. But when her stomach had started to grow and that little bump had appeared it had been impossible to deny the fact that somehow on that one night together she and Dec had made a baby.

"I know. I guess it must have not worked. Believe me, I went over that night in detail a million times. For a while before DJ was born I almost wished it had never happened. I'm never that impetuous."

"DJ?" he asked. He leaned forward, and some of the fear was leaving his eyes and she thought she saw him starting to plan.

She didn't want to give him too much time to think because Dec off his guard worked for her. Dec making plans and convincing her to go along with him... Well, let's just say that was what landed her in this position.

"Yes, I named him Declan Junior, but I've always called him DJ so no one in the family would suspect who his father was. Since this is California I didn't have to name a father on the birth certificate, and as far as my sisters are concerned, DJ's dad was a one-night stand. Someone whose last name I didn't get."

"I think they might put two and two together once I start—"

"No. You don't start anything. I'm telling you about him because you're here now and there might come a time when DJ wants to get to know you." She got that he had rights to his son but she'd seen so many fathers really screw up their kids—her own, for example. And she wasn't about to take a chance in letting DJ start to care and count on Dec just to have him bail when he was done with the merger.

She had no reason to believe he'd do anything else. Dec was essentially a stranger to her. If she could go back in time and tell herself anything, it would be to get to know this man before sleeping with him.

"I want to know my son," he said at last. He leaned forward and stared into her eyes. "I want to meet him and have a chance to be a father to him."

"Not even thirty minutes ago you said you didn't want a family," she reminded him, because the temptation was to believe him. She still had that vision in her head of the perfect little family. She still wanted a partner to help her raise DJ. But she just wasn't sure that Declan Montrose could be that man.

Dec was reeling. This was easily the biggest shock of his life. He had never thought of having kids because he knew how fragile life was. Knew how hard it was to be a great parent—he'd had two experiences of being essentially left alone as a child. First when his biological parents had put him up for adoption. And then when Helene and Beau Montrose had brought him into their Beverly Hills mansion. They'd both had very full lives and usually just trotted him out for family photos, leaving him feeling alone, more like a well-pampered pet than a son.

Having a kid… Having anyone rely on him outside of the office… Well, it wasn't something he'd been prepared for. He'd been leading Cari to seduction, but suddenly lust had taken a backseat. And that was what had him thinking that he needed to say and do the right thing here. He still wanted her, and the thought of a child with her wasn't sending him into full panic mode.

He'd always been a loner and he knew himself well enough to acknowledge that he probably was essentially the same sort of man that he'd always been. However, for the first time since he'd left his parents' home and their fortune behind, he felt charged with a sense of purpose.

He just wasn't sure what that purpose was.

A son. The thought still made his hands shake. He shoved aside his own nerves, put his hands on the table and leaned over toward her.

"I'd like to see my son," he said again. He was going to keep asking until he saw him. Until he held him in his arms. He couldn't believe he had a son.

She nodded. "It will be easier if you and I do this on our own. Once our families are involved it will get messy."

She had no idea how messy, Dec thought. Especially when Kell found out. Kell was a maniac when it came to the Chandler family, and given that he'd grown up with their grandfather and his mother hadn't brought in an influx of cash the way that Helene had, Kell had been bitter and focused all of his energy on revenge. His cousin, who was always looking for another way to bring the Chandlers to their knees, would use DJ as a pawn. He could easily imagine Kell urging Dec to be the sole guardian of the boy so he could be raised to hate the Chandlers the way Kell had been. Dec was sure of it.

In his mind he ordered the important events that had to take place. Order and planning were how he'd managed his life, and despite the fact that Cari was sitting across from him with those big blue eyes of hers and a determined stare, he planned to take charge. In the end she'd thank him.

"I will come to your house tomorrow and meet our son," he said emphatically.

"Just call him DJ."

"Why? He's my son."

"Yes, but you're not ready to be a father."

He arched one eyebrow at her, prepared to brazen out the fact that he could be an excellent dad. But then he thought of giving up his Maserati. Thought of the fact that a baby couldn't live on a yacht. Thought of all the things that he'd used to keep his life from having a real anchor and a real home. All of that would have to change....

"I am willing to try," he said.

She nibbled at her full pink lower lip and tipped her head to the side to study him. She was searching for something, and he tried to look earnest and not desperate, but he couldn't shake the fact that for the first time since he'd been brought into the Montrose family, he truly had flesh and blood of his own. He and his cousins were united in purpose, but they knew the same way Dec did that he wasn't really a Montrose. Now, though, he had a son. Someone who belonged to him. No one ever had before, and when he was alone he'd explore these unfamiliar feelings coursing through him for the first time.

The full importance of the moment hit him hard in the gut and he gripped the table to keep locked in this moment. He wasn't alone anymore. But this woman was the key to access to his son. He knew nothing about her except the sounds she'd made when she'd been in his arms.

"Trying is good," she said.

To be honest, he had no idea what she was talking about. Only knew that she was willing to give him a chance, and that was all he needed. "Okay, so I will come by your house tomorrow morning."

"I have to pick him up from Emma's first thing and then we can meet at the beach."

"Why the beach?" he asked.

"DJ likes it there. Plus my housekeeper will be at home and her sister is Emma's housekeeper. I want to keep this between you and me for right now. I don't want DJ to be part of what's been going on between our families."

"Agreed," he said. "When I said I wasn't ever having a family, that was just me trying to keep you from knowing that I wanted you."

She gave him a knowing look. "Yeah, right. That was you warning me that you weren't planning to stick around this time either."

That was exactly what it had been. And he was glad that she wasn't looking to him to be something he wasn't sure he could be. A part of him wanted to be upset with her for not instantly seeing him as part of her little family, but another part of him was relieved. Maybe he could be like a favored uncle to DJ?

But he knew that wouldn't satisfy him. Knowing he had a son was making him think of things that had never seemed important or that he'd never thought would be applicable to him. Suddenly he wanted to visit that mansion in Beverly Hills that he'd inherited when his mother had died eight years earlier. Suddenly he wanted to hold his son in his arms and show him how to be tough enough—no, to protect him so he didn't have to be tough enough to survive in the world. He knew that he wanted that little boy that he'd only seen on Cari's phone to grow up without the issues and fears that had dominated his own life.

"I'm sorry, Cari. You probably did the right thing by keeping our son a secret," he said.

"I did the only thing I could," she said.

"Now that we both know we have a son, I will be able to help you with the decisions," he said.

"I don't need help," she said.

"What do you need?" he asked, knowing he was going to have to be cooperative and to try to convince her he possessed whatever traits she deemed necessary for her son's father. Because the more he thought about DJ, the more he realized that for the first time since he'd left home and started helping Kell acquire and break businesses apart, he wanted to build something of his own. He wanted to build something that would last with his son. He wanted to build a family.

Cari wasn't too sure exactly what she needed except to get home and to get away from Dec. He was trying and that was one of the sweetest things she'd ever seen him do. Okay, it was definitely the sweetest. Dec wasn't a man who asked. He normally bullied and pushed until he got what he wanted.

She knew that she'd thrown him a curveball and she should probably get him to agree to as much as he would tonight. But she hadn't counted on it feeling like a curveball to her, too. She'd thought he'd deny the existence of a son. She'd feared he'd just shrug and walk away. But this reaction was the one she'd secretly hoped for.

In her mind's eye she could just imagine Jessi shaking her head and telling Cari to snap out of it. And Cari knew that Jess would be right to say those words. Dec was still the same man he'd been earlier. She had to remember that people didn't change in less than an hour.

Dec was a man who destroyed things. He was the axman for Playtone Games and there were probably hundreds of people whose lives he'd altered with the cold-blooded decisions he made every day. It was silly to think he wasn't going to apply those same principles to his personal life.

"I guess I should be going. If you don't want to take me back to the restaurant, I can catch a cab."

"Why would you say that?" he asked her.

"I figured you need some time to process everything I said tonight."

"I definitely do, but you're not catching a cab," he said. "We have to start getting to know each other."

She nodded. "That's why I came to dinner with you tonight."

"That, and guilt," he said.

She couldn't help but smile at the knowing way he'd said that. "Maybe."

She hadn't realized what a heavy emotional strain

keeping DJ a secret had been, but for the first time this evening she felt able to breathe and that knot of tension in her stomach had loosened.

"So tell me… Well, tell me about how you first took the news," he said. "It had to have been a shock."

She leaned back in her chair and she remembered she'd gone to the walk-in clinic in Vegas where she'd been for her last gaming trade show. The news that the doctor had delivered had been more of a confirmation of what she'd sort of already guessed. "Immediately I knew I couldn't tell anyone who you were."

"Why not?" he asked. "Are you close to your sisters?"

"We are sort of close. When our parents were alive, our dad was busy working and our mom had her moments when she was unavailable to us. So Emma and Jessi sort of looked out for me," she said. "I wanted to tell them, especially since Emma already had a son, but I was afraid and unsure. And I had this little baby inside of me and I knew that I was all he had."

She almost touched her stomach, remembering the very instant when she'd made the decision to keep the baby's father a secret from her sisters. Dec hadn't called and she'd felt like it was her and the baby together against the world. "I just knew that I had to protect him and keep him safe. From that moment forward I did everything for him."

He was watching her like he'd never seen her before, and she couldn't blame him. She didn't have to be a rocket scientist to know he'd wanted the evening to go in a different direction. And he was handling it as Dec handled everything.

"Does nothing throw you?" she asked.

"This did," he admitted. "I have always been so careful and never planned or anticipated a child."

She smiled. "DJ surprised us both. I said something similar to Jessi when I was decorating the nursery a few weeks before he was born and she said that maybe there was something in the universe that had a different plan for me."

"Do you believe that?" he asked.

"I can tell you don't. But a part of me would like to think that what happened between you and me was more than just hormones going crazy. That even though one night was all you really wanted from me there was something more going on there. I know I sound like a hopeless romantic," she said.

"I'm not romantic," he said. "I think the condom malfunctioned and we have a son. Nothing more was involved in it. But I do think what you and I do with him, how we raise him, how we treat each other, those are the things that will have a long-lasting effect on him."

"I agree," she said. "Which is why until I say otherwise, we're going to keep the fact that you are DJ's father a secret."

He didn't look too happy about her decision but she really didn't care. She wasn't about to risk her son or herself falling for a man who was used to leaving. Who was used to always having one foot out the door.

"Okay, but you and I will date."

"Why? Whatever for?"

"It's the only way to get our families used to the fact that we are together. And eventually they are going to learn about me and DJ. Don't you think it will be a lot better if we give them a chance to get used to me first?"

He had a point.

"I don't think so. We should keep this just between us."

But her sisters were going to give her the third degree. Even so, she was tired of keeping the secret of DJ's father. And it looked like she was going to have a chance at the family she'd always wanted with the only man who'd ever kissed her and made her forget everything but the way she felt in his arms.

Six

Dating. Dec wanted them to date and Cari had left him with a vague nod of the head, but had been careful not to agree to anything. There was no way that their families were ever going to accept them as a couple. Emma and Jessi would have a lot to say about her dating a Montrose.

Especially given the way that Dec had been sent to evaluate and chop up their company. No matter what spin he tried to put on it, everyone knew he was there to break up the company in payback for her grandfather cutting old Thomas Montrose out of Infinity all those years ago.

She rubbed her bleary eyes as she stared at the digital numbers of the clock. It was three-thirty and she doubted Emma would appreciate her showing up to pick up DJ. But she needed her son home in her arms.

She'd made a bad choice in allowing her sister to take him to her home.

Tonight she needed to hold his warm little body close and breathe in his sweet baby scent and remind herself that she could be strong. Instead she was lying in her big bed and dreaming of Dec. Was it any surprise?

She hadn't forgotten their one night together. Since then, no other man was interested in her. And to be honest she wasn't interested in any other man. Was she interested in Dec?

Attracted to him? Definitely. More than that? She just didn't know him well enough to be sure. The parts she'd seen had shown her a man who was ready for a good time and serious about business, but there wasn't much else she could say about him.

Perhaps his dating idea was a good suggestion. She'd have a chance to get to know him and see if he was really the right man to be a father to DJ. It didn't matter to her that he'd provided the sperm. In a very basic way she almost felt as if she'd gone to a sperm bank.... Why hadn't she thought of that lie to tell her sisters?

Jessi already suspected that DJ's father was someone they knew. She was always asking sly questions and trying to pry the name out of her. And if Cari hadn't been so determined to keep her secret she would have given Dec up long ago.

She rolled over and punched her pillow into shape, wrapping her arm around it and closing her eyes. It was only her inherent weakness where he was concerned that made her imagine she was curled against Dec with her arm around his chest.

She didn't even pretend she was thinking of any other man. There was only her in the bedroom and she wasn't about to lie to herself. She was weak where he was concerned and she really had to remember that he was just a man. And he was flawed.

He was a commitmentphobe. Sometimes she was frustrated with herself for never doing anything the easy way. It would have been so much better to fall for Jacob, who worked for the accounting firm that did the independent audit of their books each year and who was always asking her out and who, as he'd told her numerous times, wanted to start a family.

But she wasn't attracted to Jacob. He was safe and a little boring. To be fair, he was a lot like she was and she had always wanted someone a little dangerous. But danger didn't seem fun or exciting now as she lay alone in her bed and wondered how she was going to keep herself from painting Dec as the man she wanted him to be.

Even tonight when he'd said to stop the blame game, she had looked at him and seen guilt and maybe some pain. But as the man who drove a Maserati and told her he didn't want a family, he might not be thinking that he wished he'd known about his son sooner so he could have been with them.

She rubbed her head and tossed, turning over one more time. Biting back a scream of frustration at the way her own thoughts kept circling and making her crazy, she climbed out of bed and went into her home office. She turned on her Eiffel Tower desk lamp and sat down on her padded chaise before grabbing her iPad and pashmina. Time for a little retail therapy. Nothing cleared her mind like shopping did.

And right now she needed to get out of her own head.

But when she turned on her iPad she saw DJ's smiling little face. Those big brown eyes of his looked up at her and she wondered how she could hard-line Dec and keep him out of DJ's life if there was even the slightest chance that he could be the father she hoped he'd be.

She traced her finger over her son's face and knew that no matter what she had to protect him. The best thing to do with Dec and his dating plan was to keep it platonic.

But that wasn't going to be easy. It hadn't taken much for him to get her blood stirring and make her breasts heavy and full. She wanted Dec. Her body felt empty and aching. She wanted to just have more mindless sex with him, but she wasn't stupid. If the last time had had life-changing consequences, this time was even more dangerous.

She had to keep her head together. She opened the Safari web browser and saw the Mommy & Me class page was still open. She'd just signed herself and DJ up for swimming lessons. She leaned her head back against the wall and closed her eyes.

If anyone had told her that a man would have this much influence over her life she would have called him or her a liar. But even though he wasn't her boyfriend and hadn't been in her life for over eighteen months, Declan Montrose was surely the one who was driving every choice she made.

Dec waited at the entrance to the Santa Monica Pier where Cari had said she'd meet him. He'd grown up taking Saturday trips here with his nanny until he turned ten and his mother had decreed him too old for the amusements. Now as he stood in the mid-August sun on a weekday waiting to meet his own son for the first time, he wondered if he should just give Cari a check to help her out with any child-rearing expenses and walk away.

His mother should have done that. She just hadn't had it in her to be kind and caring, and she'd even told him when he'd asked her why she'd adopted a child that she'd done it so that Thomas Montrose couldn't get his hands on any of her fortune. She'd started to become bitter about being married for her money. He rubbed the back of his neck and shook his head.

"Dec?"

He turned and saw Cari standing a few feet from him. She was dressed for the office in slim-fitting black slacks that she'd paired with a sheer, flimsy-looking long-sleeved blouse. He could see the outline of her bra underneath it. But his eyes were focused on the baby in her arms.

She stood there sort of uncertain, and then she pushed her sunglasses up on her head and smiled at him.

"I knew you'd be here early," she said.

He realized she was nervous, and he thought back to that boy he'd been so long ago and how he'd never been sure around his parents. Never sure that they loved him and really wanted him. Then he looked at the baby in Cari's arms and felt a surge of love for him.

"This is DJ," she said when he walked over to stand next to her.

Dec looked down at his son and felt that strong surge of emotion again, and tears burned his eyes. He kept his head down so she wouldn't see. He'd never felt anything as powerful as he did at this moment. "Can I hold him?"

"Of course," she said. She turned the baby in her arms and handed him over to Dec.

Dec hesitated, feeling awkward and unsure, and the baby made a little noise as he took him into his arms. "Hey there, DJ."

"Mamamama," he said. But it wasn't clean or crisp.

His little mouth moved on the word and drew it out. His little hands reached up and Cari snatched Dec's sunglasses a second before DJ's hands got there.

"Sorry, he has a thing for sunglasses and I don't think you'd appreciate him chewing on these," she said.

"It's fine," he said. He was caught up in the fact that DJ was his. Of all the things he'd achieved in his life, this was the most unexpected.

"Want to walk up the pier?" she asked.

"Sure."

"You okay?" she asked when they started walking.

He nodded. He wasn't ready to talk about any of his emotions with Cari or anyone else.

DJ wore a one-piece romper-type suit made of cotton and he smelled like baby powder. His little hands moved on Dec's shoulder as he carried the baby so that they faced each other. Finally he just had to stop and look down at the boy who was muttering different little sounds.

He had a son.

Sure, he'd known that last night, but holding the boy in his arms today made it real. Until this moment he'd been able to think of the future and his own plans, but now he knew that he was going to have to consider this little boy and make sure he was safe and secure. Looking down into his face, he realized he wanted to be a better man.

He never thought or measured himself by anyone else's standards. He'd learned early on that he couldn't please others easily and settled for pleasing himself. Now, though, he wanted to make sure that in DJ's eyes he was always a hero.

The little boy stared up at him and one of his hands came up to touch the side of Dec's face, and he could only look down into that round sweet little face. His own son humbled him. Yet even as he was thinking about how DJ had his eyes, he saw Cari's little nose and that DJ's blond hair came from her, as well.

He glanced around and saw her standing a few feet away, taking a picture with her cell phone. She was giving him privacy to get to know his son and recording this moment for DJ, he guessed.

"Mamama…"

Dec turned to Cari.

"He sometimes means me, but usually he just mutters that a lot," she explained.

"Oh, so what does he do?"

"Mostly what you've observed. He talks and chews on his hand. He does get fussy but I just fed him and changed him so he'd look good for you," she said, coming over to them. "Wanted my little man to look his best when he met you for the first time. What do you think?"

He was humbled. "You did good, Cari."

She laughed. "I had a lot of drugs to help with the birth."

"Did you? I want to hear about that."

"Now?"

He shook his head. "Let's go get some breakfast and talk about what we're going to do now. I'm not sure what you're thinking but I would really like to be a part of his life."

"Okay, let's go talk," she said. She wasn't worried about her sisters seeing them since it was the middle of the morning on a workday.

He led the way to a coffee shop with outdoor seating and reluctantly gave DJ back to Cari to go order some coffee and muffins for them. He watched her through the glass and noticed that other men watched her, as well. She was very attractive, and even holding the baby wasn't a detriment to other men seeing her and wanting her. Dec had to fight against his own jealousy for the first time ever.

He wanted to walk out there and claim both the mother and child as his own. That scared him because he wasn't entirely sure he could have them both. Or what he'd do with them for the long haul. But he knew he had to find the answer to that soon.

Cari had seen a different side to Dec when he'd held DJ for the first time. She was trying hard to remember that right now he wanted everything to work out, but once life got back to normal he might not want anything long-term. He was thirty-five years old, enough to have settled down before this, but had never found a reason to. He was still a bachelor for a reason and she knew it was because he was, in his own words, a loner.

"Decaf latte," he said, placing it in front of her before he sat down across from her at one of those tiny tables that all coffee shops seemed to specialize in. His long legs stretched out on either side of her own as he tried to get comfortable.

Nearly impossible for a man as big as Dec. He was almost six-four. She wondered if DJ would be as tall one day.

"Thank you," she said.

"You're welcome." He took a sip of his drink, which looked like a double espresso.

"My thoughts are pretty straightforward on this," he said. "I want to start dating you and get to know you. I'd like to also spend time with DJ but not necessarily always with you. I want him to get used to me."

She narrowed her gaze on him. This was where she

had to be sure and remember she was DJ's mom. She couldn't give in the way she sometimes did at work. "Do you know anything about kids?"

"No," he said. "But I'm a quick learner."

"What I'm thinking is that you can come to our house and spend some time with DJ. That way I'm close by in case something goes wrong. Would you be agreeable to that?"

"At first, but I want him to get used to being at my place," Dec said.

"Where do you live?" she asked. "I have a place in Malibu."

"Right now I have my parents' mansion in Beverly Hills, but I usually stay on my yacht at the marina."

"I'm not sure—"

"I know a yacht isn't the right home for a baby. I'm meeting a Realtor after work to look at condos."

He was already changing, she thought. But having a baby wasn't always going to be like this. There were times when DJ started crying and nothing would soothe him. How would Dec react to that?

"We'll just play that part by ear," she said.

"Fine. But I'm letting you know that I want to have him at my place eventually."

She nodded. When he was thirty, DJ could go wherever he wanted.

"Now, about dating," he said matter-of-factly. "I don't want this to be a fake thing."

"Do you have a checklist?" she asked.

He scowled at her. "As a matter of fact I do. I've… This is the first time I've been around an actual blood relative," he said. "I don't want to screw it up."

She felt her heart melt. She wanted to be careful and

tried to picture him as the Tin Man again, but it was hard when he was earnest like this.

"Okay, what's next on your list?"

"I want to get to know you."

"I want that, too," she admitted.

"Good. There's more… I still want you." He reached out and touched the side of her face and she felt a shiver go through her.

"I had already figured that part out for myself," she said. It hadn't taken a brain surgeon to realize that the lust that originally brought them together was still sparking between them. "I want you, too, but I'm not sure if that's just because you're forbidden fruit."

"Forbidden?"

"Well, you are my family's enemy."

"Was that part of why you went out with me initially?" he asked.

"Uh, no. I didn't realize who you were until we were partway through dinner."

"What? How did you not know what I looked like? We grew up with flash cards of you guys," he said.

"Please tell me you are kidding," she said. "I'm picturing something akin to America's War on Terror cards."

"I am joking. But how did you not recognize me?"

"I just always pictured Thomas Montrose when I thought of your family. We have that portrait in our building."

"So after you realized it was me—your 'mortal enemy'—what did you think then?"

"Don't let this go to your head, but you can be very charming when you want something," she said.

"I know," he said with that arrogant grin of his. "So we'll date now and see where our relationship goes?"

"What if it doesn't work out?" she asked. "Will you still see DJ?"

"Yes," Dec said. "I'm not sure what kind of father I can be, but I want to try to be the best I can for him. He deserves to grow up knowing his dad wanted him."

"Being wanted is important to you?" she asked.

"You know I'm adopted, right?" he asked.

She nodded. They'd never talked about it and she wondered if he felt awkward about it.

"Well, I always knew my biological parents didn't want me."

"But your adoptive parents picked you," she said. She had a friend who'd adopted last year and Gail was always sure to let her toddler know that she loved her even more because she'd been chosen.

"I guess. But there is always that doubt that I'm good enough because my biological parents didn't want me."

She nodded; it explained a lot about how hard Dec worked and how he was always moving on to the next goal. She even thought that he might be a really good dad if it meant that he could keep DJ from feeling that way. But knowing that was what he wanted wasn't enough. He was going to have to prove himself with his actions before she'd really trust him.

"Okay. So this dating thing, how is it going to work?" she asked.

"As you know, this is a busy week at work for us. I believe you have a game that is supposed to be delivered," he said.

"Yes," she said. "Maybe we should wait until next week?"

"No, we can have a late dinner tonight. I'll stop by when I'm done for the day and see how your day is going," he said.

That he was willing to accommodate her schedule made her feel pretty good. "That would be nice."

"Where does DJ go during the day?"

"The nursery at Infinity. I usually bring him up to my office after hours and let him play in the corner while I finish working."

"I could pick him up," Dec said.

"No. My sisters would know you had and that would raise questions," she said.

"How would they know?"

"Emma has a three-year-old son who is in the day-care facility, as well," Cari said.

"Okay, then I will bring dinner to your office and we can all eat together," he said.

She wasn't sure how it had worked out that Dec had gotten everything he wanted from her. He had merely amped up the charm and she'd succumbed. In the future she had to be more careful. She wasn't going to make things too easy for him. After all, he was the guy who had wanted her for one night and then walked away. While she was the first to admit having a child changed people—it had changed her after all—she still didn't trust Dec.

She'd keep her eye on him and try to ensure that she didn't lose any more of herself than she already had. It would be a hell of a lot easier to manage if she didn't like him.

Seven

Cari tried to focus on work while she was at the office, but she had a steady stream of appointments from employees who all wanted to talk about Dec. Though they wanted to discuss the future and what Cari thought he was going to do with their roles in the company, she had no answers. She told Ally to hold her calls and escaped upstairs to the executive floor where Emma's office was.

The decision to move her office down onto the development floor had made sense when Cari had taken over the role of COO. She wanted to be where the staff saw her every day and where she could see what they were working on. The move had paid off and she and the staff had a good rapport.

"You look like you are on the run," Emma said when Cari got off the elevator. Her sister wore a severe-looking business suit and had her thick black hair pulled back in a bun. Her usual corporate look. Cari didn't envy Emma at all. As the oldest, the responsibility of keeping Infinity going had fallen to her.

"I am. Are you leaving?" she asked Emma.

"Yes. I have a lunch meeting across town," Emma said, glancing down at her watch. "Should I cancel? Do you need me?"

Cari remembered when she was seven and used to be scared at night. She'd creep down the long, dark hallway to Emma's room—her parents had a firm no-sleeping-in-our-room policy—and she'd stand in the doorway next to her sister's bed and whisper her name until Emma would roll over and lift the covers, inviting her into the bed with her. Emma had always been the one she ran to when she had a problem.

And it was so hard now to not tell her everything. Even harder than it had been before Dec had come back into her life. She wanted to lean on someone else, to unburden herself so that the responsibility of the decision wouldn't be hers. But she knew she couldn't do that. Inside she sighed, but outside she smiled at her sister.

"I'll always need my big sis, but I don't want you to cancel your lunch plans. The staff is in full panic mode. I just needed to escape where no one could find me," she admitted, which was partially the truth. She couldn't work with the steady stream of people coming to her office to ask questions every five minutes.

Since she'd worked her way up to COO she'd always had an open-door policy. She'd learned from her time at the different levels in the company that most of the staff needed to be heard more than they needed action.

"Well, you are welcome to use my office. I'm out until two," Emma said. "Sam wanted me to tell you that he's happy to babysit DJ whenever you need him to."

"Really?"

"Yes. He's trying to teach him to say 'what's up, dog?'"

"Why?"

"He thinks it will crack you up," Emma said. "He told me about you both doing hip-hop on 'Sing Star.'"

"That was supposed to be a secret," Cari said. But remembering playing the singing game with her nephew made her smile and she thought of all that Emma had been shouldering since her young husband had died. And Cari knew that if Emma could do it, so could she. Hiding out wasn't a Chandler trait. Cari knew that no matter how much she wanted distance, she could not run from Dec.

"Thanks, Em."

"You're welcome, sweetie. Are you sure you don't need me?"

Cari gathered her strength around her and stood taller. She was an adult, an executive, and she didn't need to rely on her sister anymore. She couldn't keep running away or hiding from the tough things in life. "Of course. Thanks for caring."

"Can't help myself since I'm always right. I like to show off," Emma said with a cheeky grin.

"As if," Cari said. "I think I just need a break. Thanks, sis. I'll ride down in the elevator with you."

The ride in the elevator was short, but when she got off Cari felt like a changed woman. So much had been out of her control since Dec had arrived, not only the takeover but her own personal life, though she realized that it was only her perception. She was still the confident woman she'd grown into since the birth of her son. Having Dec back here, just down the hall from her, changed nothing.

"I thought you were out of here," Ally said when she walked back into the office.

"I just needed a break," Cari said. She knew the takeover was hard enough on her staff without her running every time things got tough.

"Changed my mind," Cari said. "I think we need an all-staff meeting. Send a global email and tell them to meet in the cafeteria at two this afternoon. Get the cafeteria staff to set up cookies and sodas. I'm going to introduce Dec and talk about the takeover. I will take questions but only on general topics."

"Are you sure you want to do that? People are acting crazy," Ally said.

"I know. That's why we need to do this. Maybe if we get it all out in the open it will be better."

"All what?"

"That there will be staff reductions and the best way for them to save their jobs is to do them instead of coming to me," Cari said. "I'm going down to talk to Dec."

"I think Mr. McKinney is in there with him," Ally said.

"His cousin? Why is he here?" Cari asked.

"I don't know. Perhaps we should bug the conference room," Ally said with an arched eyebrow.

"I don't think that's a solution," Cari said.

"Well, it would make it easier to find out who is on the chopping block," Ally said.

"It's also illegal."

"Picky picky," Ally said.

She just smiled at her assistant as she went into her office to gather her thoughts before heading down to see Dec. She jotted down some business questions about reduction targets and the deadline to make all of them. But as she stared down at her own handwriting, she realized she had other questions. Maybe that was why she was so restless.

She wanted to know what he expected from dating her and if he'd be kissing her again. And as soon as she identified what her true worries were, she felt better. She wanted him, and this morning seeing him holding DJ had only made him more attractive to her. He didn't seem like a loner or a man who would abandon her a second time.

And that was very dangerous thinking.

Dec leaned back in the leather chair he'd had brought over from his office at Playtone and looked at his cousin, trying to gauge why he'd stopped by. Allan was thirty-five like Dec but was two inches shorter and looked a lot like the Montrose family with his thick dark hair and silver-colored eyes. He was an avid outdoorsman and always had a tan, not hard to achieve in California.

"Why are you here?" Dec said when they finished discussing the current lineup of the Lakers. The cousins had season tickets to floor seats and were anticipating a good year when the season started. "I doubt you came over here to discuss the Lakers."

"Too true. Kell thinks you're tired from Australia and don't have your head in the game," Allan said.

"Why does he think that? I've been sending him reports since I hit the ground. He's just anxious and acting like a maniac."

"I agree. But I told him I'd stop by and check it out."

"Well, you have, so I guess we're done."

"Not yet. The assistant to the COO practically glared a hole through me."

"It's safe to say the staff aren't happy that we've acquired them. Some of them are downright belligerent but I can handle it. Most of the companies we take over are the same," Dec said.

"But Kell feels so personal about this one," Allan said.

"I know," Dec said, pushing his chair back. "Do you? I know that I'm kind of not as involved in the rivalry as you both were. I mean, my mother could have cared less what happened to Gregory. She saw her money as the solution."

"It was a solution, but not the one Grandfather ultimately wanted," Allan said. "I think your dad was sick of the rivalry, too. That's why—"

"He married an heiress," Dec filled in. "I know it is. He said as much when he was drinking. Why couldn't the old man let it go?"

"He wasn't built that way," Allan said. "And neither is Kell."

"Well, he's going to have to give some ground on this. The days of coming in to a hostile takeover and firing everyone are gone. Especially in our industry. We'll end up alienating a lot of potential talent," Dec explained. "Some of the staff here are guys we want making games for us."

"I get it," Allan said. "I don't envy you this job. Why do you do it?"

"What do you mean?"

"We both know you don't have to work, you never have had to," Allan said.

Dec couldn't put it into words, but it made him feel like a real Montrose to be a part of the company. To do his part to help his cousins achieve their goal of revenge against the Chandlers. He'd always been on the outside until that day when he was twenty-three and Kell had called and asked him if he wanted to start a rival game company to beat Infinity in the marketplace. "I'm a Montrose."

"True dat," Allan said with a grin. "How's the Chandler girl you're dealing with?"

Incredible, Dec thought. There was no way he'd reveal to Allan his true feelings for Cari when he didn't even have a handle on them himself yet. But as an executive, she was actually doing a good job of giving him the space he needed to evaluate the staff. "She's good."

"I know the middle sister, Jessi."

"You do?" He remembered Kell mentioning a night of drinking and something about Allan and the middle sister. "Since when?"

"About two years now. Her best friend is married to my best friend," Allan said. "Every time they have a major event, there she is to annoy me."

"Is she serious about the rivalry?" he asked, because from what he could tell, Cari didn't really let it bother her too much.

"She's serious about being a pain in the ass. She had John investigated before the wedding."

"You're kidding. He comes from one of the oldest moneyed families in the country," Dec said. They were distantly related on his mother's side.

"I know, right? She said that money didn't make someone a good person," Allan said.

"Was she doing it just to needle you?" Dec asked.

"Probably. She gets under my skin."

"I know what you mean," Dec muttered under his breath.

"Woman troubles? I didn't even think you were dating anyone," Allan said.

"I might be dating," he said as the conference room door opened after a brief knock before he could say anything else. He glanced up to see Cari standing there. Her straight hair was pulled back in the high ponytail she habitually wore it in, with the fringe of bangs falling straight on her forehead. Her blue eyes looked quizzical.

"Sorry to interrupt, but I needed to talk to you about a staff meeting."

"Glad to have the interruption. Do you know my cousin Allan?"

"I do not," she said, stepping forward to shake Allan's hand.

"You seem less hostile than your sister," Allan said.

"I try," Cari said with a wry grin. "She's not overly fond of you either."

"I was totally aware of it, since she is usually scowling when I walk into a room." Allan let go of her hand. "You don't look anything like your sisters," he said.

"I know. They used to tell me I was adopted when we were little," she said.

"And I really was," Dec interjected. "We have so much in common."

Dec noticed Allan's glance flicking between him and Cari. "Interesting," his cousin commented.

"What's interesting?" Cari asked, looking slightly confused.

"Nothing," Allan said.

Dec stepped toward his cousin. "Allan, don't you have to leave?"

"Not yet," Allan said. "I'm here to observe, remember?"

The situation wasn't ideal in Dec's mind. He didn't want his cousin watching him and Cari together. But he knew there was no way he was getting Allan out of here short of throwing him out.

* * *

Cari had hoped not to see Dec's cousin, but it served to remind her of the other players in this game. It was hard not to look at the entire situation the way she did when they were building a game. It was easier to think of Allan as an adversary that had to either be swayed to join her team or destroyed.

In her mind she'd clothed herself in armor and a shield before coming down to the conference room and she was very glad she had. She realized that she had to keep the "dating" part of her life under very careful control. There was something about Dec and this entire thing that made her wish the timing was different.

Would she have been able to save Infinity if she'd sought Dec out when she'd first learned she was pregnant instead of waiting? She doubted it. Families didn't end feuds just because of marriages or heirs. World War I had certainly proved that, she thought.

"What can I help you with?" Dec asked Cari, breaking into her thoughts.

"It's the staff. They are all so anxious. I'm going to hold a general staff meeting this afternoon and I'd like to give them some information to ease their fears," she said.

"What are your ideas?" he asked.

"I'd like to have a hard target for your reduction. Just something like twenty percent of staff or thirty percent off the bottom line for expenses. Something concrete for the staff to know that if they work at it then they will be safe."

Allan leaned forward and looked up at her. "Sit down, Cari."

She sat down on the other side of the table from him.

"Do you really think knowing that will help the staff?" Allan asked.

"Yes. My group is really good at meeting financial targets. We all know reductions need to be made and by going to the staff in the past I've been able to achieve them. I want to make this transition easier on them. Right now if you looked at our efficiency, you'd see that in one day we're off track. They are all worried."

"Well, we don't have a hard target in reductions yet," Dec said. "I'm still gathering information to take back to Allan."

"I'm the CFO," Allan said.

"I know," Cari said. "We believe in knowing our enemy. And according to Jessi you have cloven hooves and a tail."

"She's the devilish one," Allan said.

Cari bit her lip to keep from smiling. Her sister and Allan didn't get along at all. "What kind of reductions in expense would make you comfortable?"

Dec glanced at Allan. There seemed to be some sort of unspoken communication going on between the men. She leaned back in her chair and noted that Dec was the more attractive of the two men. Sure, Allan had those California outdoorsy good looks, but he didn't affect her the way that Dec did. As she studied Dec, she noticed the tiny scar underneath his left eye that she hadn't noticed before.

And his mouth… Well, she'd done a lot of thinking about that full mouth and the way his lips felt pressed against hers. The way he opened his mouth and thrust his tongue into hers. From their very first kiss, she'd noted how he tasted good.

"Will that work, Cari?"

Damn. She'd been daydreaming and she'd missed

something important. So now she either had to pretend she agreed with whatever they'd just discussed or admit she wasn't paying attention. Being a blonde, she'd always felt at a disadvantage in discussions like this because people assumed she didn't get it. That she wasn't as smart as everyone else, and now she'd just acted like a fool and proved it.

"Let me see what you've worked out," she said.

Dec nodded and passed her the legal pad on which he and Allan had jotted some numbers down, and as she studied it she saw that if her division could move firmly into a 20 percent profit margin, then no one would have to be cut from the operational group.

"I can work with that," she said. It would mean long hours and getting their games in early. In fact, as she stared at the numbers she had an idea that might do more than save jobs. It might give Playtone a reason to keep Infinity in business.

"Glad to hear it. That's a very aggressive number," Allan said. "I don't know many divisions of any gaming company that could do it."

Dec spoke before Cari could reply. "Well, you haven't seen Cari in action. I've spent the past two days listening to every staff member tell me she's the best boss they've ever had. I think they'd kill themselves to please her."

Cari rolled her eyes. "He's exaggerating. It's just that I'm empathetic."

"It's more than that," Dec said. "There's something special about you."

She felt her cheeks heat up with a blush and shook her head. There was that glimmer in Dec's eyes that had nothing to do with her business acumen and everything to do with the bond between them. And whether it lasted or not, she realized there was always going to be that strong attraction between them.

"Well, I don't know about that. But I will do my best," she said, standing up to leave.

"I'll see you for dinner," Dec said.

"I'm looking forward to it," she said, smiling at him before turning and walking away.

She hoped that Allan would see a woman who was confident and knew what she was doing instead of a bundle of nerves who might have bitten off more than she could chew. Even the metaphorical armor she was mentally wearing felt tattered, but more from the inside than from any outer blows. It was going to be hard to keep these two parts of their lives separate.

Because she wasn't used to separating her emotions from any of her decisions. And Dec was certainly a man who made her feel emotional.

Eight

Dec ordered a dinner from his favorite restaurant for delivery at seven. Since the first evening they'd eaten together in Cari's office almost two weeks ago, it had become his favorite time of the day. Most of the staff was still present, but as he approached Cari's office he noted that her assistant was gone. He stood in the doorway watching her sitting on the floor with DJ.

DJ noticed him in the doorway, rolled onto all fours and crawled over to him.

"Uh, hello, Dec."

"What are you trying to teach him?" Dec asked, putting the take-out food on the credenza and reaching down to pick up his son. He felt that kick in the chest again from the thought that this was his progeny. He hugged DJ and the boy smiled up at him and made a grab for his nose. "Mamama."

"No," Dec said. "Dada."

"Mamama," DJ said.

"He's stubborn, must get that from—"

"Watch it, buddy," Cari said, getting to her feet.

"I was going to say me," Dec said, carrying DJ over to the desk where she had set his carrier. "Is he sitting here while we eat?"

"Yes. I have some yogurt in my fridge for him. Do you feel comfortable getting him settled?"

"Sure," Dec said. He might be new to this dad thing, but with Cari close by he figured he could handle it. Besides, there was little in his life that he hadn't been able to figure out. And this was no different. When he'd first struck out on his own he'd had nothing but his wits to guide him, having refused to touch the money his parents had wanted to give him, and his desire to prove himself. And he'd done a damned fine job of it.

"Do you need a hand?" she asked as she came back with the yogurt.

He'd been staring at the car seat instead of putting the baby in it. He got him in and fastened the straps before turning to the dinner he'd brought for them. "Mind if I close the door?"

"Not at all," Cari said.

She started spoon-feeding DJ mouthfuls of yogurt, and the little man didn't look too thrilled with that. "Are you sure that's good for him? He's a boy."

Cari rolled her eyes as she looked over at him. "I think I know what my son needs."

He held his hands up in a truce motion and went back to setting up their dinner. "I guess I'm a little jealous of all the bonding you've already done with our son and I hardly know anything about him. I didn't even know he'd like yogurt."

"Well, he loves chicken, too," Cari said. "I can see

FREE Merchandise is 'in the Cards' for you!

Dear Reader,

We're giving away FREE MERCHANDISE!

Seriously, we'd like to reward you for reading this novel by giving you **FREE MERCHANDISE** worth over $20. And no purchase is necessary!

You see the Jack of Hearts sticker above? Paste that sticker in the box on the Free Merchandise Voucher inside. Return the Voucher promptly...and we'll send you valuable Free Merchandise!

Thanks again for reading one of our novels—and enjoy your Free Merchandise with our compliments!

Pam Powers

Pam Powers

P.S. Look inside to see what Free Merchandise is **"in the cards"** for you!

W

e'd like to send you two free books to introduce you to the Harlequin Desire® series. These books are worth over $10, but they are yours to keep absolutely FREE! We'll even send you 2 wonderful surprise gifts. You can't lose!

REMEMBER: Your Free Merchandise, consisting of **2 Free Books** and **2 Free Gifts**, is worth over $20.00! No purchase is necessary, so please send for your Free Merchandise today.

Plus TWO FREE GIFTS!

We'll also send you two wonderful FREE GIFTS (worth about $10), in addition to your 2 Free Harlequin Desire books!

Visit us at:

www.ReaderService.com

YOUR FREE MERCHANDISE INCLUDES...

2 FREE Harlequin Desire® Books

AND 2 FREE Mystery Gifts

FREE MERCHANDISE VOUCHER

2 FREE BOOKS and 2 FREE GIFTS

Please send my Free Merchandise, consisting of **2 Free Books** and **2 Free Mystery Gifts**. I understand that I am under no obligation to buy anything, as explained on the back of this card.

225/326 HDL F42Z

Please Print

FIRST NAME

LAST NAME

ADDRESS

APT.#   CITY

STATE/PROV.   ZIP/POSTAL CODE

NO PURCHASE NECESSARY!

▼ Detach card and mail today. No stamp needed. ▼

© 2012 HARLEQUIN ENTERPRISES LIMITED. ® and ™ are trademarks owned and used by the trademark owner and/or its licensee. Printed in the U.S.A.

HDL-FM-08/13

you have a lot to catch up on. Are you sure you want to put in the effort?"

He looked at her and wondered what she was getting at. The first stirrings of anger moved through him, but then he looked down into her eyes and saw an emotion that looked like fear in them. He had to remember that he'd left her. After one night.

"What are you thinking?" she asked.

"That I wish you'd told me about him before he was born," Dec said with all the emotion he felt. "I feel like you cheated me."

"I know I did," she said. "I can't even say I'd do it differently now. Given that we had a one-night stand and you weren't easy to find…it just seemed like maybe I was meant to keep DJ for myself."

"I can understand that," he said, and that was a big part of why he was conflicted. He also felt that she was fully justified to have some doubts where he was concerned. "I do want to. I don't know if I'm changing or what this is, Cari, and you have every right to question me. Because every time you do it just reinforces my own desire to be here for my son."

She gave him a tentative smile. "Good. I intend to."

She wiped DJ's face and then went back to the refrigerator, heated the milk in the microwave and returned with a bottle.

"Is he on formula?" Dec asked.

"No. It's milk I expressed earlier," she said. "It's easier to keep to my work schedule if I do it this way."

She handed the bottle to DJ who took it and started sucking on it. A few minutes later his eyes started to drift shut. "He's like clockwork. After he eats he needs a nap."

"I guess that's a good thing for us tonight. Our dinner is ready," Dec said.

"Let me move his seat to the floor where I can keep an eye on him while we are eating," she said.

Dec watched as she got their son comfortable, putting a stuffed toy next to him and tucking a blanket around him. "I hate to leave him in the seat, but when I'm working late it's easier on him if he sleeps in here until I'm ready to go."

"Do you work late often?" Dec asked.

"Well, not to make you feel guilty—"

"You can't."

"I have only been working long hours since we got wind of the takeover," she continued as if he hadn't interrupted.

"I'm sorry you've had to. I could have warned you there was nothing that was going to keep Kell from his goal once he fixed on it."

"I'm not surprised. Stubbornness seems to be a Montrose trait."

"I'm a Montrose in name only."

"You were raised by them, Dec. Why do you always point out that you are different?" she asked.

"I've always felt different," he said. "It wasn't anything anyone said to me per se, just my own feeling that I had to work a lot harder to prove myself."

"Why? I've done some searching on your family and without your mom's money Thomas Montrose wouldn't have had any chance of reviving his game empire."

Dec looked over at her. It was odd to him, but it felt like she had just defended him and his right to be a Montrose. It wasn't like she'd said anything he hadn't already known, but hearing someone else with that opinion made the difference.

"That's all true, but I always felt like I didn't fit in," he said.

"I'm sorry," she said. "I didn't keep DJ from you because you didn't 'fit' my idea of a father. I just wasn't sure enough of myself to invite any other complications into the mix."

He nodded. He could see that. She was a good mom and her love for DJ was evident. He hoped someday that he'd be part of that circle of people she cared for.

Cari learned a lot about Dec as they dined after she'd taken DJ down to the nursery where the day-care staff were on extended hours. They had cribs and DJ was much more comfortable sleeping there than in his car seat. Plus she wanted a chance to have Dec to herself and figure out what she was going to do with him.

It was as if it were their first date. He didn't talk any more about his past. But she felt as if for the first time they were on the same track.

There was still an undercurrent of desire between them. Every time she looked over at him and caught him watching her she felt her blood flow a little heavier. And when their hands brushed, tingles ran up her arm and sent a delicious shiver through her entire body. But tonight was about more than sex. It was about getting to know each other. She wondered if perhaps it was fated that they do things out of order.

"What are you thinking?" he asked, breaking into her thoughts.

"That I'm finally getting to know the real guy you are," she said.

"That's not true. You've seen me naked. You know the real me," he said.

She shook her head. "You're wrong. Today I noticed this for the first time."

She reached over and ran her forefinger over the small scar under his left eye. "Where did you get that?"

He brought his hand up and caught hers, carrying it to his mouth for a brief kiss. "That scar is from when I was nine. It was the first time I went camping with my grandfather and Kell and Allan. They'd both been going with him since they were six, but Mother and Grandfather had been feuding so I hadn't been able to attend until that summer."

"What were they feuding about?" she asked. Seemed old Thomas had a beef with everyone.

"Her money," Dec said. "So when we got to Bear—"

"Big Bear?" she asked. "My maternal grandparents had a house up there."

"Yes, Big Bear," he said. "Am I going to be able to tell this story?"

"Sure, but with lots of interruptions," she said with a grin.

"So we got up there and my cousins were already expert snowboarders, but I had never been on one. I knew how to ski because my mother insisted I learn when we were in St. Moritz the previous winter. But Kell said skiing was for wimps so I asked for a snowboard and then proceeded to lose control and run into a tree. I had a lot of damage to the left side of my face and had emergency cosmetic surgery. This scar is all that's left."

She hadn't been expecting that. She reached over and took his hand in hers and rubbed her fingers over his knuckles. She felt for that little boy that Dec had been. Desperate to prove himself to the Montroses and find his place. "Can you snowboard now?"

"Nope. Just ski and I don't care if Kell thinks it's for wimps. He felt bad because he'd sort of dared me into taking the snowboard."

"You were just boys. Your grandfather should have stepped in."

"He thought that kind of thing was good for us. He said we should always stay hungry."

"Well, I don't agree with that. I'm not raising DJ that way."

"Good. I'm not complaining about the way I was raised, but I want DJ to have a more comfortable childhood than I did."

"Is that why you are trying to have a relationship with me?" she asked.

"Part of it. I don't want him to ever think that I didn't want him. I know how I felt knowing that my biological parents... Well, that's old news. What about you? Any scars?"

She didn't want to let the subject change. She wanted to know more about Dec and dig into his psyche, but she could tell he wasn't going to answer anything else about his past.

"I have one scar and if you guess where it is—"

"I get to kiss it," he said.

"Why would you want to?"

"So it's some place naughty?"

She just shook her head. "No."

"Ah, okay. And I can kiss it if I guess correctly?"

"Sure," she said. There was no way he'd guess it.

"Stand up," he said.

"Why?"

"So I can make a thorough examination of you. How am I going to make an informed decision without all the evidence?"

She rolled her eyes and realized that Dec wanted to keep things light between them tonight. So different from his usual serious and brooding manner. And so she pirouetted for him. That took a little of her joy from the evening. He was letting her see the parts of himself he deemed okay and keeping the real man hidden from her still.

And she was being her usual open book. She knew she had to change, but how? She wondered if there was a way she could learn from Dec. Maybe stop letting her heart be so open....

"The back of your knee," he said.

Her eyes widened and furrowed her brow as she looked at him. "Yes. How did you know that?"

"It was a guess."

"No way," she said, glancing down at her legs covered in trousers. "Confess."

"I'm guessing you're going to renege on the kiss," he said.

"No. We made a deal. I just want to know how you knew."

"I saw you naked, Cari," he said. "And I've revisited that night many times in my mind. Don't think for a minute that I didn't memorize every inch of your lovely body, from that scar on the back of your knee to that strawberry birthmark at the base of your spine."

She melted. That he'd remembered those details...it meant nothing. All it meant was that he was a thorough lover, which she already knew. But it felt like it meant something more to her tonight.

She looked at him and felt that sinking feeling in her stomach as she fought against doing something she shouldn't. Instead she lifted her hand and beckoned him to her with one crook of her finger.

He stood up and walked over to her slowly. She stopped him when he was a few inches from her with her hand on his chest. "I can't decide if you are a big flirt, a serious lover or the biggest mistake of my life."

"I am a big flirt and will always be serious about loving you. As for the other, this doesn't feel like a mistake to me," he said, pulling her into his arms and kissing her.

There was nothing light or tentative in the way that Dec's mouth moved over hers. His hand on the back of her neck was strong and he held her where he wanted her as he ravished her mouth. He was aggressive and strong, taking what he needed from her, giving her what she hadn't known she craved until this very second. Every move of his body seduced her into letting go of her own reservations and giving in to her need, as well. His tongue teased hers with a parry and retreat until he thrust it deeply into her mouth. His hands soothed their way down her back to her waist as he drew her in closer to him.

She felt the muscled strength of his chest and his pecs under the crispness of his dress shirt. She felt the tension in his fingers as he squeezed her waist and drew her up off her feet and against his body. She felt his hardening erection and knew that for tonight the games had ended.

There was no playing around with this kind of lust, and she didn't want to. She'd told him about his son, they were slowly working out how to deal with their companies and it had been a long eighteen months for her without sex. Without a man's hands on her body. Not just any man—this one.

She wrapped her arms around his shoulders and toyed with the hair at the back of his neck. He angled his head to the left to deepen their kiss and she knew she wanted more. She sucked on his tongue as he tried to withdraw it from her mouth. He smelled of man and musk and Dec. It was a scent she'd thought she'd never smell again and though she'd been trying so hard to pretend this was no big deal, she was so glad he was back in her life.

She tore her mouth from his, looking up to meet his dark brown gaze. His skin was flushed with arousal and the look in his eyes was so intense she shivered from it. He lowered his mouth again and this time the hungry kiss was slower, more sensual, deeper.

She stopped thinking, just let herself give in to the passion that he drew so easily from her. He lifted her again, his hands cupping her buttocks as he shifted his hips to grind his manhood against the apex of her thighs. He hit her in the perfect spot and she let her head fall back as his mouth moved down her neck.

"Wrap your legs around my waist," he said against her skin, his voice a gruff, husky sound that made her quiver.

She did as he asked and he carried her across the room to her walnut desk. He set her on the top of it. She kept her legs wrapped around his waist and lifted her hips against his erection, rubbing herself against him.

He put his hands on either side of the desk next to her hips. "Lean back."

She hesitated.

"Do it," he said.

She did, propping herself up on her elbows. He started to undo the tiny black buttons that lined the front of her blouse. Slowly he undid the first one and then leaned in and dropped a kiss on her exposed flesh. Then he moved to the next one and then the next. He stopped when her blouse fell open enough to reveal her bra.

"I seem to remember lace the last time," he said.

"My breasts are a lot bigger now."

"Yes, they are," he said, cupping the left one and stroking her nipple with the side of his forefinger.

Her breasts felt full and her nipple tightened and she felt a bit of wetness as a little milk came out. He rubbed his finger over it and then reached beneath the fabric of the bra to rub her naked flesh.

She wondered if that would shatter the mood. It didn't for her because she was on fire for him. And she needed him now. He lifted one hand to touch her almost reverently and she glanced up at his face. He still had that intense look of desire, but it was teamed with the softest expression she'd ever seen on his face.

"Not sexy at all," she said.

"Maybe not to another man, but it's a reminder to me of what we share," he said.

She wanted to ask him more about that but he leaned down and kissed her. This time wasn't as fierce as it had been earlier but it was just as intense. She was overwhelmed by an upsurge of tenderness from him as he drew her closer to him and continued to deepen the kiss.

"Sorry," she said, not sure how to stop her breast from doing that.

"Don't apologize," he said, continuing to unbutton her shirt.

She reached for his shoulders and drew him closer to her, wanting to embrace him so she wouldn't feel so vulnerable, but he kept the distance between them.

He looked deep into her eyes and asked, "Do you still want me?"

"Yes," she said, knowing she could hide nothing from this man. "Yes."

Nine

That was the response he'd been waiting for.

Growling her name, Dec reached between them for the fastening of her pants, undoing the button and then lowering the zipper. She shifted her hips as he pushed one hand into the opening. Then his mouth came back to hers.

Everything about Cari was more tonight. Her perfume lingered in his senses with each breath he inhaled. Her skin felt softer than before, and the new weight from carrying DJ filled out her curves. He loved every new thing he discovered about her.

He realized that no matter what it was he thought he knew about her, he hadn't really known her at all. The way he felt right now, like he was going to explode if he didn't get inside of her, made him regret that he'd put his business first. He should have stayed in her arms. He pushed should-haves out of his mind and concentrated on the way she tasted on his tongue.

He pushed his hand farther into her panties, letting one finger trace the humid warmth at the opening of her body. She said his name on a breathless sigh and he smiled down at her. She shifted against him, her hand finding first his thigh and then the hard length of his erection. She stroked him up and down through the fabric of his pants, holding on to him and rubbing her finger over the tip.

She fumbled for his zipper and he reached down and opened his pants, freeing his length. She gripped him and drew him closer to her, reaching lower between his legs to cup him.

He parted her with his fingers and she closed her hand tightly on his erection as her hips canted up toward him. This was a remembered pleasure. The way she responded to his touch. As lovers, they both heated up together, and he felt at this moment they were completely in sync.

He continued to explore her feminine secrets but was frustrated by the fabric of her pants, which trapped his hand. He used his free arm to lift her off the desk. "Shove your pants off."

She did as he asked and when they were on the tops of her thighs he set her back down on the desk and lowered her pants and panties to the floor, removing her shoes at the same time. He put his hands on her thighs and pushed her legs open, leaned down over her. He breathed in the feminine scent of her and then dropped nibbling kisses on the inside of her thigh, moving higher until he bit lightly at her hip bone.

She shifted and put one hand on his head and the other on her stomach. He saw that her belly had a slight curve to it now where before it had been flat, and he noticed the faint stretch marks on her skin. Every sign that she'd carried his baby just turned him on more and more. It enhanced his need to claim her again.

His child had left its sign on her and now he wanted to, as well. He lowered his head to bite the inside of her thigh and then he licked at the spot and kissed it gently before turning his head to her center. He'd not forgotten the intimate taste of her and he craved it again.

He parted her with his fingers and rubbed his tongue over the taut bud there. Then he suckled her gently into his mouth. She shifted under him, and he held her still as he continued to feast at her most intimate flesh and then slid his hand under her thigh to trace the opening of her body again. He entered her with just the tip of one finger, and her hips jerked against him until he slid it farther inside her and then brought it back out.

He moved his face lower and thrust his tongue deep inside of her. Her hands came to his head and held him to her as her hips canted upward toward him. He knew she was on the edge. Could taste it on her and feel it in the way her body was softening for him. He pulled back and pushed his finger in deep, and then up to find her G-spot.

She made a high-pitched keening sound as her hips thrust against him and he felt her body tighten around his finger. He kept his hand on her and in her, rocking it against her until she collapsed backward on the desk. He stood up, looking down at her, and smiled at her as she opened her dazed eyes.

"Thank you for that," she said.

"It was my pleasure," he said.

"No, it was mine. It feels like a lifetime since I've felt like that," she said to him.

"How long has it been?" he asked.

"Eighteen months," she said, looking up at him with

those clear blue eyes of hers. "I've been sort of busy, and most men aren't interested in a new mom."

"Good." He didn't want any other man in the picture. He felt possessive toward both her and DJ. They were his.

His.

Yes, he decided. She was his and he didn't have a clue about how to keep her or what he should do with her beyond sex, but he knew that he wasn't going to let her go. It didn't matter that she was way too innocent for a man like him. He had claimed her. Well, almost.

She reached for his manhood, which was still rock hard, and stroked him with her hand. As she leaned down toward him, he felt the brush of her breath against him and the touch of her tongue. Then, with a shiver down his spine, he felt a drop of his essence slip past his control. She licked it up and then took him into her mouth. He put his hand on the back of her head, stroking her blond hair.

He wanted to enjoy every second of her like this. He tried to pull back to warn her that she needed to stop, but she put her hands on his backside and kept him where he was. Her mouth moved over him until his hips jerked forward as his orgasm rocked through him.

She took him deeper into her mouth until he was totally spent. When he pulled back he didn't know what to say, but Cari didn't give him a chance. She just sat up, pulled him into her arms and rested her head right over his heart. And he held her in his arms, letting all the worries of whether he was the right man for this woman disappear. For tonight at least he wanted to enjoy just being in her arms.

* * *

Cari didn't have words right now or the strength to pretend like this was nothing more than sex. And she was so afraid that Dec would just leave her like he had the last time. She hadn't realized until this moment that the fear was still inside her, just under the surface of the confidence that she now recognized as bravado instead of strength.

She twisted her head and looked away, hoping to keep her emotions hidden from Dec. She saw DJ's car seat and it brought back the fact that the last time she'd been in this man's arms her entire life had changed. And though she was on the pill, she wasn't ready to risk another unplanned pregnancy.

She shifted away from him and hopped off the desk, gathering her underwear and slacks with as much dignity as she could muster.

"I'm going to pop into the bathroom. Be right back," she said, walking away before he had a chance to respond.

She closed the door to her private washroom and locked it before putting down the toilet seat and sitting down. A million different emotions roiled through her. Of course, pleasure still saturated every nerve of her body, but she had to keep blinking to stop the tears that burned her eyes from falling.

She wanted tonight to be real. Not just the sex but the dinner and the quiet conversation. She wanted it badly with every part of her being and it worried her that she might just be making it into something it wasn't.

What if she walked back out there and he was casual and blasé about what had just happened? How was she going to play it? She wasn't cool or sophisticated when it came to him. Any other man... Well, hell, any other man wouldn't have made her feel what Dec did. It was just him, and she was slowly coming to realize that she wanted more from him than she'd believed she could get.

He was trying.

But she needed more than trying if she felt this strongly. She needed him to be someone that she wasn't sure he could be. And she had the sinking feeling that she was setting herself up for heartache.

There was a knock on the door.

"You okay?"

"Yes, sorry. Just a few more minutes."

"I've got to go wash up. And then I'm going to go and get DJ from the nursery. That will give you some time to yourself."

"Okay."

She needed both the time and the continued privacy. She stood up, realizing she couldn't hide in here forever. She washed up, got dressed again. Her hair had slipped from her ponytail and she took it down and then slowly put it back up as she stared at herself in the mirror.

In movies and on TV people always seemed to convey conviction and determination with a look, but she couldn't. The more she tried, the more fearful she was that tonight had been a mistake.

It was too soon for things to be sexual between them. He was still adjusting to having a son and she was still adjusting to him being back in her life.

She opened the door and found the room empty. She cleaned up the dishes from their dinner and noted that Dec had left the baby carrier behind. She put it back up on the table and got all of her stuff together so she was ready to go home when they returned.

Her cell phone rang and she glanced at the caller ID to see that it was Emma. "Hey, Em."

"Hello, am I interrupting anything important?"

"No. I just finished a late dinner and am getting ready to head home. What's up?"

"I was thinking more about the idea you emailed me this afternoon, the one about getting a second game out in this quarter so that we can increase profit to meet the financial targets that Allan set."

"I've been thinking about it, too," she said. It had been playing second fiddle to Dec all afternoon and evening. And Emma's call was just what she needed to get her mind back where it needed to be.

"Well, how do you feel about contacting Fiona? You know she was on that matchmaking show last year with Alex Cannon. You are still friends with her, right?"

Hardly, Cari thought. She'd met Fiona McCaw-Cannon at a UN summer camp when they were sixteen and for three years they had been pen pals. Not exactly the kind of relationship that warranted a call to ask her new husband to come bail them out with an award-winning game design. "I'll see what I can do, but I'm not counting on that. I was thinking that we have our IOS team take our existing first-person-shooter game and turn it into a Christmas game for the iPad and Android tablets."

"How will that work?" Emma asked.

"I thought we could change the target into a house or a tree and then have the game player decorate with a holiday gun? It's just a first thought, but it would be a holiday game, and that is a lucrative market."

"Yes, I like it. I'm going to send a meeting request to you and our project board. This sounds like the beginnings of just what we need. Use our existing assets."

"It will save the bottom line, and I have to run it past finance, but I bet we wouldn't need to sell too many to make a profit."

"Good thinking. I can't wait to discuss this tomorrow. Thanks, Cari."

She said goodbye to her sister and leaned back in her office chair, wishing that she could solve the problem between her and Dec as easily. But games were much easier for her than real life because they were just that—games.

Tonight everything was going his way, Dec thought as he entered the nursery and retrieved his son from Rita, the day-care nurse who was on duty tonight. He carried the boy back toward Cari's office. DJ was chortling happily, making that "dada" noise again and Dec felt like he was king of his world. There hadn't been a lot of times when he'd been filled with… He didn't really know what this was. He wasn't a miserable son of a bitch generally, but he also wasn't happy. But tonight he felt the first seeds of what he might be.

It was scary, though, because when he'd held Cari in his arms he'd had that soul-deep fear that if he let go of her she might disappear. He knew she wasn't like him and wouldn't just walk away like he had, but another part of him feared she would. It would serve him right if she did, but he was praying that he could show her… What?

She was going to need more than sex from him, and he'd never been good at emotions. He hadn't been lying when he'd told her he'd left that morning after to avoid the messy stuff. Now here he was wanting it…almost. He'd seen the fear in her eyes as she'd dashed into her private washroom. Carrying DJ tucked against his chest and seeing those sleepy brown eyes watching him now, Dec felt the weight of his actions.

He almost wondered if he should propose to her. Get her to marry him. And then what? Being married wasn't going to be a solution to the problems that still existed between them. A marriage license hadn't been a magical cure-all for his parents' problems, and he knew better than to suggest that to Cari tonight.

He just had to find the right words to say. And the right way to say them. And then maybe they would be able to move on from here. What he really wanted was to take Cari and DJ to his yacht and then sail off for the horizon. But that was taking running away to the extreme and he couldn't do that. Not now when he was finally really part of the Montrose legacy.

He wasn't the outsider he'd always been. And Cari wouldn't leave her sisters now anyway. He knew that without even asking her.

He paused in the hallway that led to Cari's office. Saw the awards on the wall and the photos of the staff that were hung there. DJ reached out toward one framed picture and Dec realized it was of Cari, Emma and Jessi with their grandfather. This family was part of his son's heritage.

At that moment he realized how important it was that he save both hereditary lines for his son. And he had no idea how he was going to do that. Kell wasn't going to be satisfied if any part of Infinity Games still existed when the takeover was completed.

He shifted the boy to his shoulder and continued down the hall, stopping in the outer office when he heard Cari on the phone. Her exact words weren't clear.

He rapped on the door before pushing it open and noticed she sat behind her desk with her arms crossed over her chest. He remembered her nakedness and wanted her again. The orgasm he'd had was nice but he knew he wasn't going to be satisfied until he made her totally his again. Until he'd taken her and claimed her once again for himself.

He needed that. And he hadn't realized how much until this moment when he saw her defensive posture and realized that while tonight had eased some of his concerns, it had simply heightened hers.

"I guess you are ready to go home?"

"Yes. It's late and I have an early-morning meeting," she said. "Besides, DJ needs to be in bed, too."

"I think his nap helped him," Dec said.

"You're right," she said, reaching for the boy.

Dec dropped a kiss on his son's head before handing him over to her. "I know."

She moved around the office, busying herself with getting ready to leave. She slung her laptop case and the diaper bag over one shoulder and then balanced DJ on her hip while reaching for the car seat.

"I'll get that. In fact, I can carry your bags, too," he said reaching for them.

But she pushed his hand away. "It's okay. I can get it all. I'm used to doing it on my own."

The words weren't meant to be a jab at him, but he felt it all the same. She was used to doing it on her own because he'd left her. He wondered if her mood had anything to do with the fear that he might do it again. And what kind of reassurance could he give her? Just the fact that he still wanted her. That he had never felt this way before. That if he could, he'd stay with her forever. Even though he usually didn't think of himself in those terms—forever.

"I think we need to talk."

"Not tonight," she said.

"Yes, tonight," he countered. He reached past her, took the bags from her shoulder and placed them on the table. "I don't like the way you're acting."

"I'm sorry you don't. I'm not sure how to change it right now."

"I am," he said walking back to her.

But she put her hand up. "Stop. Sex isn't going to fix this."

"I didn't think it would. I was going to give you a hug, Cari. I thought you might need some reassurance that this isn't like the last time."

"I know it isn't, Dec. We have a son now."

Ten

"Yes, we do. I've been trying to ease my way into your life, but it's not enough, is it?" he asked. He had no idea how to build a relationship. Or anything for that matter. He was an expert on breaking up companies and parceling off different parts of them. He was an ace at walking away before things got too hot and heavy. And here he was trying to convince the one woman who knew him best that he wanted to change.

She shrugged, and it was like an arrow to his heart. He knew that he wasn't fooling her. There was not going to be an easy way for him to ease into this. Half-truths and grand gestures weren't going to win her over. He was going to have to convince her of his sincerity.

She nibbled at her lower lip as she shook her head. "I don't know. Tonight was nice and I really enjoyed it until that moment when—"

He didn't understand what she meant. He silently

cursed his adoptive parents, who'd shipped him away
when he was old enough to start walking and talking.
Even though they hadn't been close, it would have ben-
efited him to have at least observed them interacting
together. Maybe he would have gleaned something he
could use now with Cari.

"What moment?" he asked.

She nervously pushed a strand of hair back behind
her ear and then rubbed her cheek against DJ's head.
Dec noticed that she held the baby closer and cuddled
him like she drew strength from having their son in
her arms.

"Cari?"

She sighed. "The moment that I realized I didn't
know if you were going to stick around. Or if it was
going to be like last time…and I know I told you I
changed, and I have, but I also care about you, Dec. It's
not love, I'm trying not to be too emotional or messy,
but you're my baby's father and it's hard not to care."

Dec took a step back, not knowing what to say. He
rubbed the back of his neck and cursed the wonderful
legacy of his upbringing that had left him so hollow
and empty inside that he ended up hurting this woman.
He was trying to be what she needed, but he saw now
that it was going to take a lot more than just trying to
make her happy.

"I thought you knew that now I'm trying to find that
bond with you," he said. He didn't want to have to talk
about what he wanted. Or how a part of him wanted
her to fill that emptiness that had been inside of him
for too long.

"I don't know. All I know is that I didn't want to let
you go, but I can't hold you either. I'm not sure if you're

just enthralled with the newness of having a blood relative of your own or if this is something real."

She'd hit the nail on the head with that observation and he shouldn't be surprised. She was astute, and her staff had spent the better part of the week telling him she was empathetic. She'd want to ease his suffering to make this easier on him, but she had to keep her guard up because of who he was.

"I do want a bond with you, Cari. I can't make you promises because I know how easily they can be broken. But I'm trying. Can that be enough for you? For now?" he asked. He'd wanted so little in this life, nothing that had caused this ache inside him at the thought of losing her. Tonight when he was alone he needed to examine this new weakness. This kind of caring was a detriment to a man in the middle of taking over a company. This was the worst possible time for her to be making him suddenly feel emotions.

She tipped her head and studied him. Something he noticed she did when she was weighing options. He hoped he measured up, and did his best to look sincere. He thought he saw doubt and maybe some disappointment in her eyes, so he furrowed his brow as he looked over at her.

"You look like you might punch me if I don't say yes," she said at last with a sad little half smile.

"That was me being sincere," he said. He wasn't even good at that. How the hell did he think he was going to manage a commitment to her and to his son? He was going to have to be in touch with his feelings and express them. Or would he? His own father never had, and Dec had scarcely known the man. He'd wanted to have fun with him, to have a closer bond.

She shook her head and gave a little laugh. "You

shouldn't look so fierce if you want people to think you are sincere."

"I can't help it. Ever since you walked into the conference room I haven't felt blasé about a single thing. From the moment you came back in to my life nothing has been normal."

"Uh, thanks?"

"I meant it as a compliment, but it's clear to see you didn't take it that way. I'm not good at this type of conversation. Should I leave?"

She walked over to him, still holding little DJ on her hip, and put her hand on his chest over his heart, where her head had rested earlier. Even though he didn't know what he was doing, somehow he felt he was bumbling his way through this. He was doing what he needed for her to see that she was important to him.

"Don't leave. I'm so afraid that I'm giving you credit for trying harder than you really are. I don't want to be stupid where you are concerned again."

"Well, I don't want to go anywhere."

"Really?" she asked.

"Yes," he said.

She took a few tentative steps closer to him and he watched her trying hard to pretend that she hadn't just made a huge leap forward in her estimation.

The staff picnic at Infinity Games was held in mid-September. A lot of people weren't too happy with Dec because they'd had to work harder and longer than they ever had before. But everyone had heard the news, thanks to the figures she'd forwarded to the staff, that all their efforts were paying off and they were projected to be over their profit targets. So the mood on the campus at the barbecue tents was pretty upbeat.

"Davis actually smiled at me when he took his plate of food," Dec said to her with a wry grin as the last of the group of staff moved on.

"He doesn't like you, but he told me yesterday he understood that the bottom line was important," Cari said.

She and Dec had the first shift at the hot-food tent. It was a catered event but Infinity Games executive staff had always been the ones to serve the food. She had started the tradition.

It had been a little over two weeks since the night in her office, and they'd been on dates and really taken their time to get to know each other. She still felt there were times when Dec was keeping part of himself in reserve, but on the whole she was happy to have him in her life. Emma and Jessi had thought she was nuts to have gone out with Dec. But they'd both backed off when Cari had told them that he made her happy. Which was mostly true. He also made her scared and paranoid and neurotic. She didn't know why he was afraid of commitment and had done her level best to be cool and not too clingy. But each day, as she fell a little more in love with him, she had to fight her own instincts harder.

"So this is the famous cyborg of Playtone Games."

At the sound of her sister's voice, Cari looked up, sensing Dec tense beside her.

"I don't even need an introduction to know that you are Jessi Chandler," Dec said, turning to greet her sister, who looked funky in her minisundress that she'd teamed with a pair of combat boots.

"Jess, he prefers to go by Dec rather than cyborg," Cari said, going over to give her sister a hug and whisper in her ear, "Be nice."

Jessi just gave her a wink. "Ah, trying to blend in with the humans?"

"Indeed. Is there a point to all of this?" Dec asked Jessi.

"Just wanted you to remember that the staff are people with lives and jobs and had no part in anything that Gregory Chandler might have done to Thomas Montrose," Jessi said.

"He's a fair man, Ms. Jessi," Frank said, coming up to the serving line. "Good afternoon, Mr. Dec, Ms. Cari."

"Hello, Frank," Cari said, starting to make a plate of food for the security guard.

"Really?" Jessi asked Frank.

"Yes. I know most of the staff were a little scared when he first showed up, but he asks good questions, points out obvious improvements… I think most people are starting to like him."

Cari glanced over at Dec and saw that his skin was flushed and he looked distinctly uncomfortable. Jessi didn't look too pleased either and gave her a hard look that Cari couldn't really figure out.

"Thanks, Frank. Enjoy the picnic."

"I intend to," he said, walking away.

"You two are relieved from duty," Jessi said. She and her assistant Marcel walked behind the table and shooed Cari and Dec away.

Once they got out of earshot, Cari said, "Sorry about Jessi."

"It's okay. I get worse from Kell all the time. Want to grab a bite to eat before DJ gets here with your sister Emma?"

"Yes," she said. "You really made an impression on Frank."

Dec shrugged. "Six months ago I would have slated him for early retirement and given him a package of benefits, but when I talked to him I saw that he still had something to contribute here. The last thing he wants is to be retired."

"I agree. He's smart and surprisingly strong for his age," Cari said.

"How do you know that?"

"He's the one who carried my new Louis XIV side table upstairs. That thing is heavy."

Dec laughed. "Why do you like that frilly furniture so much? It's not very businesslike."

"Yes, it is. And people like it. Shows I have personality," she said. "That I'm not just another boring corporate drone."

"They don't need to see your office to know that," Dec said, glancing around them and then stealing a quick kiss. "Let's find a place to sit down."

She followed him to the picnic tables and as they approached, two of the game developers waved them over. She knew that Dec had been talking to her staff, but as she sat next to him at the table she realized he'd actually been integrating himself into the company. She didn't know if that was because he was trying to make the transition smoother or if he had another purpose.

But as she listened to the conversation flowing around her, she realized that he was a part of this group. Since observing him at the trade show a year and a half ago, she sensed that he'd changed. She wondered if it was a permanent change or if this was just his way with takeovers. She had no way of knowing for sure, she realized. She was just going to have to decide if she trusted him or not.

And as he reached under the table to squeeze her thigh, giving her an intimate smile, she knew that she already trusted him. She saw him now as a man who knew how to be a part of something bigger than himself. A man who understood that to have a successful future you had to build something, not just tear up what existed. A man whom she was glad to call her own.

Dec found a quiet spot out of the sun and away from the crowds at the picnic. Late afternoon was waning into evening and soon to come was a fireworks display and a band that would be performing as soon as dusk fell. He'd spent the day surrounded by the staff of Infinity Games. They'd all been friendly and made him feel like he was a part of the team.

He knew he wasn't. He knew that in just under two more weeks when he presented his findings to the board he was going to have to cut some of them. And the thing was, he had the feeling they knew it, too. He had never expected to care, he realized suddenly.

Takeovers weren't the place for someone who was empathetic and who couldn't keep his eye on the finances. Never before had he struggled with this, and he knew a certain blonde was to blame.

She kept expecting him to be better than he was and damn if he wasn't trying to live up to that.

But this wasn't him. He had made small talk all day long and smiled and played volleyball. And he had just reached the saturation point of being surrounded by people. He didn't want to feel vulnerable here. Business was the one place in his life where he'd always been so calm, so cool, able to keep moving forward.

But not now. Cari Chandler was changing him, and not just in his personal life.

"There you are," she said, coming up next to him.

"Mamamama," DJ said. The boy was dressed in a pair of khaki shorts and a blue Polo Ralph Lauren shirt.

"Hey there, buddy," Dec said, reaching out to his son. The boy leaned over and Cari handed him to Dec. He wished the boy would call him Dada, but he was learning that with babies and Cari everything happened in its own time.

As he cuddled his son close, some of the tension inside of him eased. "I just needed a break."

"I get that. These days can be so long. Wait until you go to the staff holiday party."

"Cari, about that," he said.

"Yes?" She looked over at him with those big blue eyes of hers and he felt a pain in his gut at the thought of saying what needed to be said.

Then he got disgusted with himself. "By Christmas, Infinity Games won't be like this."

"What do you mean?"

"You know I'm here to acquire your company. One of the things we're looking at is moving some of your staff to the Playtone campus."

She flushed and glared at him. "After today, you'd still do that?"

"Cari, that's my job."

"I thought you were starting to care."

"I am. I do care about you and about DJ."

"But not about his heritage."

Her words were quick and he understood where she was coming from. The past four-plus weeks had started a bond between them that he was reluctant to see broken, but he knew what he had to do. Kell wasn't going to give up on vengeance just because Dec had started to care about one of the Chandler sisters.

"The same could be said of you and your sisters," Dec pointed out. "The company was vulnerable. We weren't the only ones sniffing around at buying you out."

She shook her head. "We were having such a nice day. Why are you being like this?"

"Like what? This is who I am. It doesn't matter how much I like your staff. Some of them are still going to be cut. This is business."

She nodded. "I can't think like that."

"That's one of the things I really like about you," he said. "But that doesn't mean I can just give up sound fiscal thinking because I want to please you."

She crossed her arms over her chest and gave him a good hard glare. "I can't stay mad at you when you make actual sense."

He rolled his eyes. She couldn't stay mad at anyone. "That's because you're smarter than those blonde jokes you are always forwarding to me."

"They're funny," she said. "I'm sorry if it seemed I jumped on you. Is that why you are over here? Because it's hard to mingle and enjoy yourself with people you might have to let go?"

Dec didn't have the heart to tell her he just needed a break from all the people. He wasn't like Cari and wouldn't lose any sleep over the staff reductions that had to be made. The really good staff members had already proved themselves by stepping into the transition and taking the lead.

"I guess," he said.

"Sorry I wasn't more understanding," she said, giving him a quick hug.

"It's okay. Why were you looking for me?"

"To see if you'd watch DJ. My sisters and I have to introduce the entertainment and thank the staff for the work they've done this year," Cari said.

Dec realized that to her these people were extended family, and for the first time since he'd learned of the acquisition, he didn't feel good. He knew the top three names on the cut list all ended with Chandler. And as he watched this woman he was starting to care about, he realized the full impact of what that would mean to her.

"I'd be happy to watch him, but don't you think it might make people ask questions about why I am?" Dec asked.

"No one is going to be ballsy enough to question you," she said. "But if you wanted to keep hiding out…"

"I'm not hiding out, but I think staying over here out of the way of the staff is wise."

"Me, too. Thanks."

Cari leaned over and kissed DJ on the head before turning and walking away. Dec watched her make her way through the throngs of people and saw her stop and chat along the way. Though he knew they were different and he'd have no problem with losing staff, Cari was going to have a hard time when she was one of the staff who was cut.

He shifted DJ to his other arm and realized he wanted to find a way to keep her on. Because just like Frank, he didn't think Cari was going to enjoy not coming to Infinity Games every day.

Eleven

"We're here," Cari said as she parked her car in the big circle drive at the Chandler estate in Malibu.

Cari dreaded Sunday brunch with her sisters. She knew there was no way they could know what had happened in her office on her desk almost three weeks ago. They also didn't know about the dates she and Dec had been on or how without her meaning for it to happen she'd started to fall for him. But she felt like her emotions were transparent today. She adjusted the A-line slim-fitting skirt and the thick black belt at her waist as she got out of the car in front of Emma's house.

In theory they were all supposed to take turns hosting the weekly morning get-together but somehow they always ended up at Emma's. Cari liked to think it was because the house Emma lived in had been their grandparents' and of course Emma had a housekeeper who did all the cooking. But she had the feeling it was more than that.

Emma liked being the hostess. She liked being the one everyone came to. She was the oldest, and too bossy for her own good, so they let her get away with it.

She glanced at DJ, who was busy chewing on a small plastic boat that he called num-num. She got him out of the car and headed toward the house. She'd spent her weekends here as a child running on the marble floors and playing hide-and-seek in the landscaped gardens out back.

Now as she looked down at her son she smiled, thinking that he'd be doing the same thing soon. She gave him to Mrs. Hawkins, Emma's son's nanny, as soon as she entered the mansion.

She wondered what Dec's childhood home was like. He'd mentioned that he still owned it but that it stood empty. Did he have the kind of memories of his home that she did of this place?

"Sam will be glad to see this little one," Mrs. Hawkins said.

"DJ, as well. He likes playing with his cousin," Cari said.

She looked down at DJ. "You're going to see Sammy."

"Mamamama," he said up at her with that big grin of his.

She kissed his forehead just before Mrs. Hawkins scooped him up and turned to walk away. "Where are my sisters?"

"In your grandfather's den," Mrs. Hawkins said.

It didn't matter that Gregory Chandler had been dead for almost ten years now or that Emma had taken up residence here. That room would always be his.

Cari entered the heavily oak-paneled room that she

imagined still smelled of her grandfather's cigars. The large windows at the end of the room did their best to let in the sunlight but the room was still dark and felt very masculine. As a child Cari had never ventured in here as it was the domain of her stern grandfather.

"Hey, girls," Cari said. "I thought we were just having breakfast."

"We will," Emma said. Her oldest sister had thick wavy hair that she normally wore pulled back in a chignon because she said it made her look more professional. "Since Jessi is in charge of marketing I wanted to run your idea past her for the Christmas game."

"Now? I don't have any of the information with me and my staff is taking Sunday off," Cari said.

"It's fine. We'll just get a high-level rundown on it. I want to keep it a secret from Playtone until we have the finished product."

"I don't think that is going to work," Cari said. "Dec is in the office and I talked to Allan about the financial targets. If we don't show them our pro forma and some progress, I think we're in danger of losing everything."

"Why did you talk to Allan?" Jessi asked.

"He was in the office to see Dec," Cari explained. "What is it between the two of you?"

Jessi looked distinctly uncomfortable, which wasn't like her sister. "There's nothing between us. He got all protective and mad because I investigated John before Patti married him."

"Why did you do that?"

"They met in Vegas. I didn't know him, and Patti is a hot property with her business going international. He could have been a gold digger."

Cari reached over and patted her sister on the shoulder. Jessi really didn't trust anyone except those who'd proved themselves trustworthy. It made Cari a little sad because she could remember the sweet little girl that Jessi used to be before life had hardened her.

"Was he?"

"Would I have let her marry him if he was?" Jessi said, sounding disgusted. "Allan got all macho man and told me to back off."

"Just from having a private investigator look into John's past?"

"I may have also offered John a bribe to see if he'd take it and run," Jessi mumbled.

Cari shook her head and couldn't help laughing. "Oh, I'm sure that went over well."

"John forgave me, but Allan hasn't."

"Well, that doesn't matter," Emma said. "I want to know more about Cari and Dec. I know you went on one date with him the first night he showed up at the office, but scuttlebutt says you two are dating. That's not right, is it?" Emma asked.

Cari walked over to the large overstuffed leather sofa and plopped down on it. "Yes, it is right. We ended up talking about more than business at dinner and kind of hit it off."

"Hit it off?" Jessi said. "That doesn't sound like you."

"Well, it is me," she said. She didn't want to have this conversation, but realized it was exactly what she needed to do so that when she told them about Dec and DJ, it wouldn't give them both heart attacks. "I guess he just came along at the right time."

"I don't think dating him is a good idea," Emma said.

"Hell, I'm going to have him investigated," Jessi said. "Then we'll see if you can keep dating him."

"No," Cari said, standing up. "I'm sorry, but this is

my decision. I'm going to date him despite the fact that we have some history with his family."

"Does your family mean so little to you?" Emma asked.

"No, it's not like that. But men like Dec…"

"Men like Dec?" Jessi asked. "How well do you know him?"

"Not as well as you're implying, but I do sort of like him. And I haven't met that many men who I want to get to know better."

"Not since you realized you were pregnant," Jessi said.

"Yes. I don't want you two meddling in this. It's hard enough dealing with the takeover and starting to care for him. I know what I'm doing."

"I hope you do," Emma said. "Because he's not going to put you before Playtone Games. With the board meeting tomorrow morning I think it's safe to assume there isn't anything else you can do now. I just want you to be sure you know what you are doing."

Cari wasn't sure. She knew she was already putting Dec before her obligation to the company. In her mind there had to be a way for her to convince him to leave the company as it was and to keep him in her life. She wasn't going to be happy with anything less than that.

Cari believed she'd planted the seeds in his mind that he couldn't treat Infinity Games like just another business to be gobbled up. She hoped his feelings for her would lead him to the conclusion that she and her sisters and their company should stay intact.

Cari left her sister's house and drove up the Pacific Coast Highway with no real destination in mind. She had a Yo Gabba Gabba! CD on for DJ who seemed happy enough in his rear car seat.

There was no reason for the tension in her stomach. Right now she knew she was doing all she could to protect her staff from trouble at work. Right now she knew her sisters were safe and healthy. And right now she still believed that she and Dec were going to end up together and be happy.

But she knew that Jessi and Emma had planted a seed of doubt in her mind. There was no way she could just keep moving forward with Dec while not knowing what his plans were for her and her sisters and their jobs.

She knew that there was a chance—okay, more than a chance—that Dec was going to recommend that she and her sisters be cut from the head count. Everyone knew that they didn't need two sets of executives in one company who did the same thing.

But she had been hoping as the weeks had gone on that there would be a way to truly merge the different corporate entities. Today, though, she was going to have to face reality. There was no way that the Montrose heirs were going to let her and her sisters stay on.

Even worse, Cari understood where Dec and his cousins were coming from. She pulled her car onto a scenic overlook and sat there with the motor running as the truth of why her stomach hurt hit her.

She was afraid that even after he destroyed her family's heritage she'd still love him.

She hadn't wanted to admit that even to herself, but it was the truth. In fact, she loved him right now.

She glanced in the backseat at DJ and she realized that from the moment Dec had walked back into her life, she'd wanted this.

But she also wanted Dec to save her company, fall in

love with his son and love her back. She wanted him to change completely from the man she knew him to be.

And that wasn't realistic. She didn't need Jessi's P.I. to tell her that Dec didn't make business decisions from the heart. She'd called him a cyborg, and in truth that was what he was when it came to slashing the game-making companies that Playtone acquired.

She also knew that he had bonded with their son. She'd seen him on the floor playing with DJ. When he thought she wasn't looking, sometimes he held the boy close and kissed the top of his head. And she had seen that look in Dec's eyes. The one that showed how very much he cared for his son.

And he did like her. And lust after her. He made her feel like she was the only woman in the world. No matter that to him this might be something that only lasted six weeks.

She rubbed the back of her neck. In that moment she decided that she was just going to ask him flat out what his intentions were. There wasn't going to be any more guessing if he wanted her or if he was going to stay with her.

She reached into her huge handbag and took out her mobile phone, then dialed his number.

"Montrose here," Dec answered.

"It's Cari. Do you have a sec?"

"Just. I'm on my way out to play volleyball with my cousins. What's up?"

"Um…I'd like to invite you to come and have dinner with me tonight," she said. "My place six-thirty."

"I'd like that," he said. "I've got a few things I want to discuss with you."

"Me, too," she said.

"Not business," he added.

Perfect, she thought. She'd let Jessi and Emma rattle her, but she'd been spending a lot of time with Dec and her instincts where he was concerned were good. "Me, too. I'll see you later."

"I'm looking forward to it," he said, disconnecting the call.

The tension that had been in her stomach disappeared and she smiled to herself in the rear-view mirror. She needed to know where she and Dec stood and, it seemed, he wanted answers to the same questions.

The love she'd been afraid to admit to started bubbling up inside her and she had to sit in the car another minute before she started driving along. She wanted to enjoy this magical feeling inside her. Her sisters had warned her how impossible her dreams might be. Warned her that she couldn't have it all with Dec. But at this moment she realized she had to at least take a chance on him and see if her secret dreams could come true. The future she craved where she had her man, her company and the father of her son.

Dec wasn't sure how the tradition had started, but on Sunday afternoons if they were all in California, he, Kell, Allan and John, Allan's best friend, got together for a game of volleyball in Clover Park in Santa Monica. As it happened this Sunday, John was in town for the weekend. While Dec had been in Australia, John and his wife, Patti, had bought a B and B in the Outer Banks of North Carolina, after Patti had sold her interior design company for a small fortune. Dec had learned early on that it didn't matter who his biological parents were when it came to sports. No one cared as long as he was good at them. And he was. As a child, because he'd had a lot of excess energy, he'd always been signed up for something to keep his nanny from going crazy.

Kell was already there when Dec arrived wearing a sleeveless Sloppy Joe's T-shirt and a pair of board shorts. He waved when he saw Dec.

"How's it going, man?"

"Can't complain," Dec said. "It's been too long since I've done this."

"We should have come to see you in Australia," Kell said.

"Nah," Dec said with a shrug. They weren't that kind of family. "You were busy fulfilling Granddad's dream for you."

"I doubt he'd be pleased with me yet. The Chandlers are still running Infinity Games."

"Yeah, about that," Dec said. He had been slowly realizing there was no way he was going to be able to recommend that Cari lose her job. She was so much a part of the daily operation, he honestly—well, maybe his emotions were influencing him a little—thought she was necessary to the continued success of any division of Infinity.

"Yes?" Kell asked. Even though he kept his dark Ray-Bans on, Dec could feel the cold glare of his stare.

"It's just not going to be as easy as we'd hoped to separate the Chandlers from the operation."

"But you're a genius at this kind of thing. Don't sell yourself short, Dec. I'm sure you'll do what any Montrose would do," Kell said.

Dec nodded. *What any Montrose would do.* Those words haunted him. He knew how to prove to Kell he was a Montrose through and through, but he was also adopted and his mother's son. And she'd hated old Thomas Montrose more than anyone else.

Kell pulled his cell phone out. "Sorry, I've got to answer this email."

Dec moved away and let his oldest cousin get back to what he did best: business. It was clear to Dec that Kell wasn't interested in moving on from the past.

But he'd been raised by their grandfather in that old dilapidated house that Thomas had refused to move out of. His own father was the middle child and Dec had often noticed that his father never measured up. Kell's father had been killed in the first war in Iraq—Desert Storm. And there was no way Dec's dad could compete with a dead man even after he married an heiress and poured billions into the family coffers.

"Ready to get your butts handed to you, boys?" Allan called as he and John walked over to them.

"Has he been drinking already?" Dec asked as he shook John's hand.

"Just cocky as ever," John said. "Good to have you back in the country."

"Thanks," Dec said. "I've missed our Sunday games."

"You don't look like you've been sitting on your ass," Allan said.

"Not at all. I played squash in Sydney with a few boys from Kanga Games."

"Good to hear it," Allan said, reaching over to give him a slap on the shoulder. "John and I have been keeping our game strong. We're getting to be something of a legend around here."

John laughed and Kell put his cell phone away to come and join them. "Ready to do this?"

"Sure," Dec said.

A coin toss determined that Dec and Kell would serve first. Dec took the ball and went to the line. As the game progressed Dec and Kell held their own, but there was a marked difference in the two sides. John and Allan laughed and joked when they missed a shot and had the most ridiculous victory high five that Dec had ever seen.

He and Kell just got on with it and played. He wondered what made Allan so different from them. Was it the fact that his Montrose was a woman? And Grandfather Montrose had treated Aunt Becca like she was a princess instead of pitting her against her brothers?

He thought of his son and realized he wanted DJ to be more like Allan than he or Kell. He wanted his son to be happy and have friends that he laughed with.

He wanted a life of happiness, not bitterness, for the boy. And he knew that if he fired Cari there was no way DJ wouldn't someday be affected by it.

He'd never been so close to having full-blown acceptance in the Montrose family as he was at this moment, and he'd only just accepted the fact that to make his adopted family happy he was going to have to sacrifice the happiness of his own blood and his own future.

He didn't fool himself into thinking that Cari was going to stay with him if he followed the plan that would make Kell happy. And if he didn't follow it? How was he going to keep his place at Playtone?

He held a big-enough chunk of the shares to block Kell if it came down to it, thanks to his mother buying back some of the public stock, but he didn't want to make it about a power play. He wanted to find a way to make all sides realize that building the future involved a lot more than avenging the past.

And he had no idea how he was going to do it.

"Are you going to serve or just stare at the ball?" Kell asked him.

"Sorry. I just thought of something about the Infinity acquisition," Dec said.

"Don't apologize to me for thinking about crushing the Chandlers," Kell said. "That's all I do."

"All?"

"Well, I sleep, too," Kell said.

Dec felt a knot settle in his stomach. His cousins were like his brothers. The thought of hurting them was almost too much to contemplate, but he had a feeling Allan wouldn't be as upset about keeping one of the sisters on as Kell would. He was going to have to be very careful about how he managed this.

"We need to get you a hobby," Dec said.

"What do you call this?" Kell asked.

"Winning," Dec said, serving the ball and getting the last point.

"Great game," Allan said.

"Want to come back to my place for a beer?" Allan asked. "I've got some steaks and we can watch the NAS-CAR race."

"I can't," Dec said. "I've got a date."

"With?" Allan asked.

"If you must know, I'm going out with Cari."

"Cari Chandler?" Kell asked.

"Yes, we've been seeing each other."

"Is that smart?"

Dec just gave his cousin a hard look. "My personal life is personal. It's not going to affect our business."

"Unless you let it screw up your priorities," Kell said.

"Back off, man," Allan said while John took a few steps away and walked down toward the beach.

"My priorities are fine," Dec said.

"You say that now, but…we're so close to finally

fulfilling Grandfather's destiny for us. Why would you chance that for a woman?" Kell asked.

"She's not just a woman."

Kell looked like his head was going to explode. "Starting tomorrow, I will take over the transition."

"My report is finished. I have a few more notes to make but I'll be presenting it on Monday. You don't have to pull me out of my job."

"What are your findings?"

"I'd rather wait until Monday."

"I need to know that Gregory Chandler didn't pull another fast one on us in the form of his seductive granddaughter."

"She's not like that," Dec said.

"We will see," Kell said.

He walked away before Kell could say anything else, but in his heart he knew that he was going to have to choose between his past and his future. And for a man used to living in the now, that was a very uncomfortable place to be.

Twelve

Cari put DJ down for his afternoon nap at four. She'd tried to get him to sleep earlier so he'd be awake when Dec came, but he wouldn't cooperate with her. Now she was running behind on getting dinner ready.

She gave up her plans of making a roast and settled on pasta instead. It was quick and easy. Plus she knew that Dec wasn't going to suddenly realize he loved her simply because she'd made him dinner. She knew that when she was in her rational mind, but not when she was in that crazy gotta-make-him-love-me mind.

She had started an espresso granita for dessert, and since all it required was scraping the icy mixture once every thirty minutes, she was set. She rubbed the back of her neck and realized her hair was still down and probably looked a mess. She set the timer for the dessert and ran to her room.

Where was the time going? It was almost six. She

spent extra time on her hair and makeup and then got dressed in a simple sundress that showed off her arms and hid the tummy she had since she'd given birth. Pleased that she looked her best, she went back to the kitchen, but the doorbell rang before she could get there.

She took a deep breath and tried to relax. It wasn't like this one night was going to completely change her life. But she hoped it would. She'd never anticipated these feelings for Dec even two months ago. Somehow the man who'd abandoned her and left her with a child to raise had come through in a way she hadn't anticipated.

She walked to her front door to the staccato sound of her own heels and realized she hadn't put on any music. She opened the door and Dec stood there with his hair still damp at his collar, wearing a pair of khaki shorts and an open-necked shirt and deck shoes. He had on a pair of sunglasses, which he pushed up on the top of his head when she opened the door.

"Hello, gorgeous," he said. "It seems like forever since I've seen you."

"Me, too," she said with a blush. She stepped back so he could enter. He handed her a bouquet of multi-colored flowers. The bouquet was large and she glanced down at it.

"Thank you."

"I didn't know which kind you liked so I settled on this bunch of gerbera daisies because they reminded me of you."

She looked down at the yellow, pink and orange petals with their large brown centers. This was such a warm bouquet of flowers. "How do these remind you of me?"

"They make me smile," he said.

She felt a giddy rush of joy shoot through her. She

wanted to be cautious, to tell herself to slow down and not take everything he said as an undeclared admission of love for her. But it was hard. She saw him now in the new light of her emotions.

"Why are you smiling at me like that?" he asked.

"You can be very nice sometimes, Dec."

"Sometimes? I thought I was nice all the time."

She just shook her head and leaned over to kiss him. She meant for it to be a light thank-you sort of buss on the lips, but instead it turned into something more. She wrapped her free arm around his shoulders and leaned up on her tiptoes to kiss him fully.

"Wow, if this is the reaction I get to a bunch of flowers, I'm going to give them to you every day," he said.

She stepped back. The thought of him being with her every day filled her with that same bubbly feeling. She truly felt like nothing could spoil this night and that everything in her adult life had been leading to this moment. The timer started going off in the kitchen and DJ started to cry at the same time.

"DJ or kitchen?" he asked. "I don't mind helping out with either."

"Would you mind getting DJ?" she asked. She thought he'd rather spend time with his son then try to figure out what she needed him to do in the kitchen. Besides, she wanted her dinner and dessert to be perfect.

"Not at all," he said with a grin. He seemed to smile more easily these days than he had six weeks ago, and she hoped that it was because of her.

"Do I need to do anything special to get DJ ready?"

"Um…change his diaper and I laid out a little outfit for him to wear. Can you get him dressed?"

Dec nodded. "I think I can manage."

He walked down the hall and she hurried into the

kitchen, setting the daisies on the counter while she opened the freezer to scrape her icy mixture. Then she got out a vase for the flowers and tried not to let the fact that he'd brought them to her mean as much as it did.

The fact was she didn't get flowers that often. Her sisters had sent her a bouquet after she'd given birth to DJ, but before that it had been years since she'd received them. She trimmed the stems and arranged the flowers in the vase before setting it in the middle of the island in her kitchen.

Then she went back to getting dinner ready. She had assembled the ingredients for a fresh and simple sauce for the pasta with basil, cherry tomatoes and some minced garlic. She filled a large pot with water and put it on to boil, and then turned her attention to making the garlic bread.

Since she was watching her weight since she'd given birth—it was a lot harder to take off the baby weight than she'd expected it to be—she was making a low-cal version of garlic bread with thinly sliced French bread that she'd rub a piece of garlic on when it was all toasted.

She realized she was nervous about the food and the table setting and everything else, but what she really wanted was for dinner to be over and for her to talk to Dec. He'd said he had something important to discuss, too, and she hoped that after the way he'd been at the door a few minutes ago he'd tell her he cared for her as much as she did for him.

She felt the first twinge of doubt in her stomach as she realized that she desperately wanted him to love her.

Dec would have laughed in the face of anyone who six weeks ago would have said he'd be changing a diaper and getting ready to spend the night at home. It just wasn't his scene—or it hadn't been. But tonight with the homey smell of dinner wafting through the house and his ten-month-old son chattering at him as he dressed him, Dec felt like he was in the only place he should be.

That feeling in his soul of the rightness of this moment was what convinced him that he wasn't going to abandon DJ or Cari again. And that scared him because he still hadn't figured out a way to save her job. But for tonight he didn't care about games or a generations-old feud. Tonight he wanted to simply enjoy the fact that for the first time in his life he felt like he was home.

It didn't matter that technically this was Cari's house or that he'd never even been here before. He had that feeling inside that he'd always been searching for and never truly experienced. That emptiness that had been a part of him all of his life no longer felt so cold and barren.

He sat DJ up and looked at the outfit he'd decided on. He had eschewed the romper that Cari had laid out in favor of a pair of elastic-waist khaki shorts and a little button-down shirt that matched his. He wanted Cari to see that he was a part of their lives now. It was important to him that he build as much of a connection between them before the board meeting tomorrow.

He lifted DJ off the changing table and the boy squirmed to get down. Since Cari lived in a one-story Mexican-style hacienda, there were no stairs to be a danger to him. He put him down and followed his son as he crawled through the house to the kitchen.

He thought of Allan and Kell and how his cousins were still untethered to anything but their jobs, and realized that he'd changed. He knew he was going to have to make a hard decision regarding Infinity and Playtone. He also knew that he might have to make a choice.

A choice that would have seemed so simple only six weeks ago, but no longer was.

As DJ crawled into the kitchen and Cari bent over to scoop up their son and then kiss him on the head, the decision seemed to make itself.

"Oh, I like your choice in outfit, sweetie," she said to DJ. "You and Daddy match." She looked over at him with so much caring in her gaze that he felt scared.

She'd turned on her iPod while he was gone and the speaker system on the countertop played "California Gurls" by Katy Perry.

He turned away and rubbed his hands together. She'd looked so vulnerable and probably wasn't aware of it. The burden of not hurting her again felt heavy on his shoulders. "I brought some wine and it's out in the car. I'll be right back."

He turned on his heel and hurried out of her house. As soon as he was outside, he stopped halfway between the house and his car. He was torn as he looked at the Maserati parked at the curb. A part of him wanted to get in there and drive away from this entire situation.

If he left, Kell would find a way to have his revenge and Cari would eventually find a way to move on with her life. And he wouldn't have to choose between his cousin and a lifetime goal—the very thing that had defined his past—and Cari and DJ, who he knew could be his future. But he knew he wasn't going to run off. He was no coward. It was hard for him to believe he'd left Cari in a hotel room all those months ago.

A slight breeze blew down the street in the older neighborhood where Cari lived. There were hibiscus plants growing in the front yard and large palms on either side of her driveway.

He had changed, he thought. Really changed, and it was almost as if he didn't want to accept it. The change was scary because he had something he didn't want to lose. Cari and DJ. He'd never thought he'd be as vulnerable as that, but the truth was there for him to see.

He grabbed the bottle of wine and headed back into the house. He found Cari in the kitchen dancing with DJ to Olly Murs's "Dance With Me Tonight." She glanced up at him and froze mid-gyration. Something moved between them and he knew that no matter what tomorrow held he'd cherish this night forever.

"Dance with me?" she asked.

He put the bottle of wine on the countertop and took both his woman and his son in his arms and danced them around the kitchen while the catchy pop ballad played in the background. DJ giggled and Cari hummed along a little out of tune.

Just like that, everything seemed so simple. They should be together. Though it was the solution he knew he'd been steering toward all afternoon, he was very glad to have his smart little son who saw things so clearly.

He didn't know how he was going to do it, but when the dust settled at the board meeting tomorrow he was walking out of there a Montrose with the respect of his cousins, but he was also leaving with Cari.

There hadn't been much chance to talk about anything serious over dinner what with DJ there and Dec in a contemplative mood. But once she put DJ to bed and went to find Dec sitting on one of the wooden loungers in her backyard, staring up at the night sky, Cari knew the time to talk was now.

She put the baby monitor on the table before she sat down on the double lounger next to him, and he reached over to take her hand in his. "Thank you."

She gave him a quizzical look. "For what? You already complimented me on dinner."

"Thank you for my son. I didn't realize until tonight how great a gift he is. You could have made a different choice, given that I wasn't in the picture. I wouldn't have blamed you at all," he said. "And I never would have known what was missing in my life."

She felt her throat close and tears burn the back of her eyes. He would never know how hard the decision had been, given that she had been on her own and that he was her family's sworn enemy. "I don't know what to say."

"You don't have to say anything." He pulled her into his arms so that her head was cuddled on his shoulder. Then he moved around so they were on their sides facing each other.

His hands swept down her side to her hip, his fingers flexing on her buttocks. He traced a pattern on her hip and she moved a little closer to him.

"Do you trust me now?" he asked. His voice was deep in the quiet of the night.

"Yes, Dec," she said. It was nothing less than the truth.

"Good. Will you let me make love to you?" he asked. "Since we were together, I've been limiting myself to good-night kisses since that night in your office to give us both a chance to really get to know each other, but I don't think I can wait any longer," he said. He rubbed his hips against hers and she felt his erection.

"Me either," she said. She'd been aware of the boundaries between them that she'd set that night in her office, but that had changed. She wanted to be in his arms again. To be honest, it was all she'd thought about for the past few weeks. As much as she hadn't been sure she could rely on him, she'd still wanted him. After the revelations she'd had this afternoon, nothing would make her happier than to make love with him tonight.

He lowered his mouth to hers, kissing her gently but thoroughly. With only the moonlight overhead and the fragrant blossoms in the backyard surrounding them, she felt like they were in paradise.

She put her hands between them and unbuttoned his shirt until she felt the springy hair of his chest under her fingers. She rubbed her hands over his hard pecs and traced the hair as it tapered down his stomach. His belly flinched as her fingers moved lower, and he put his hand over hers.

She pulled her mouth from his and looked up at him, but he lowered his head to her neck, dropping nibbling kisses down the length of it as his hands moved down her leg to the hem of her skirt and drew it up.

With long, languid strokes of his hand up and down, he caressed her thigh. She squirmed and reached again for his belt buckle. She undid it and then struggled with the button at his waist when his hand slipped under her panties and drew them down her legs.

He rolled her over onto her back and she stared up at him in the moonlight, and in his eyes she saw the emotions she'd craved. She saw the love and the caring that she felt for him reflected back in his eyes.

He nudged her knees apart with his and settled his hips overtop of hers. It was a shock to feel the warmth of his erection against her naked flesh. He shifted his hips, lightly rubbing his manhood over her center and she felt herself moisten as she got ready for him.

He pushed her thighs farther apart and held himself poised at the entrance of her, with only the tip of his erection inside her. She shifted under him, trying to force him inside of her, but he wouldn't be budged.

She looked up at him and he brought his mouth down on hers hard, thrusting his tongue deep inside her mouth as he finally entered her fully. Spasms of pleasure shook her as he continued to thrust deep inside of her. She wrapped her thighs around his waist and urged him to move faster, with her heels against the small of his back.

She tangled her tongue with his as she felt her orgasm wash over her. She tore her mouth from his and cried out his name as he thrust into her again and again, burying his face in her neck and suckling on the pulse point as he came with a final thrust and his entire body shuddered over hers.

She rocked her hips against his one more time. He settled over her for a moment and she thrilled to have his full weight on her. She wrapped her arms and legs around him and held him with all her strength. He kissed her lightly, and when she looked up at him he was staring at her with a look of tenderness she'd never seen in his eyes before.

He rolled them to their sides, cuddled her close and stroked his hand down her side and back. She tried to shift, afraid her weight might be too much for his arm, but he held her where she was and urged her to place her head on his chest, right over his heart.

She closed her eyes as she listened to the reassuring beat of it. Being in his arms made her think that she didn't have to worry about the issues Emma had raised this afternoon. Emma didn't know Dec like Cari did. Surely a man who held her this tenderly couldn't hurt her.

Thirteen

As night deepened around them, Dec held Cari in his arms. He wanted to make love to her again. In a proper bed instead of outside on the deck chair. But he didn't regret his actions. He had waited too long to have her in his arms again. He'd thought he'd explode if he hadn't gotten inside of her.

His determination to have her and to keep his Montrose cousins happy had set his mind to turning over what he was going to do next. It was hard to think when he had Cari in his arms. He fastened his pants, found her panties and put them in his pocket so that the housekeeper didn't find them later and then stood up and lifted her into his arms.

She stirred and smiled up at him.

"I feel asleep," she said.

"Yes, you did. Now I'm ready to sleep, too…with you in my arms. May I spend the night?"

"I was hoping you would. Just promise me if you do, you'll still be here when I wake up."

He hurt inside at the fact that she had to ask that. He didn't blame her for needing reassurances. He'd done that with own actions and he was going to keep reminding her that he was here to stay.

"Yes, I will be," he said.

She picked up the baby monitor before he carried her into the house and down the hall to her bedroom.

"How did you know where my bedroom was?"

"I checked it out earlier," he said.

He set her on her feet and she put the baby monitor on her nightstand. "I'm going to wash up for bed."

"Go ahead. I'll use the hall bathroom and meet you back here."

She gave him a tentative look as she entered the master bathroom, and he looked around her bedroom while he was in there alone. He'd noticed the baby pictures on her dresser earlier. Photos of DJ from the moment he'd arrived in the hospital being cradled in the arms of a very tired-looking Cari, all the way up to a photo of him from the Infinity Games company picnic two weeks ago.

She had chronicled her son's life, and he looked at the pictures from the nine months when he'd been absent in their lives and realized that DJ wouldn't have to know he'd been missing if he handled the next few days right.

But he knew that he was also going to have to be able to give Cari what she needed from him. And he suspected sex and a dinner companion weren't going to be enough. He shoved his hands through his hair and left her bedroom to wash up. He cleaned himself and came back into her bedroom to find Cari lying in her bed.

She was propped up with some pillows behind her

back and started when he opened the door. He stood there for a second and had no idea what to do next. Sure, he'd slept with women before—hell, he'd even slept with Cari—but it had been spontaneous and naturally flowed out of sex. This was different.

He was here because he wanted to be, and he felt a little vulnerable at that thought. It reminded him of his first night in his parents' mansion and how much he wanted to stay there forever. He'd gotten his wish, but it hadn't turned out exactly as he'd expected it to. But he'd been a kid with unrealistic dreams.

"Come to bed," she said, pulling back the covers and inviting him into the room. She'd left the nightstand light turned on and it cast a soft glow into the room. He wanted to believe he belonged in there with her, but he knew that he didn't. He was darkness and she was light.

He wanted to resist her. Despite what he'd been thinking all day, his gut instinct was to turn and run. Hadn't he learned that life was easier when he didn't rely on anyone? What kind of father could he be when he was still so afraid to stay in one place?

It didn't change his feelings for DJ. He felt so much love for his son; he wanted only the best for him. And he questioned whether or not he was actually the best for DJ and for Cari.

Despite the fact that she'd filled that emptiness inside of him, he still didn't know how to commit to her. He was still thinking of the gassed-up Maserati waiting outside and how he could be halfway to Canada before the sun rose if he wanted to be.

"Dec?"

He heard the quiver in her voice and knew she must be sensing what he was feeling. The trepidation after all these weeks of building up to tonight. Now that he was here, now that he'd gotten what he wanted, he was afraid to hold on to it. Hold on to her, he corrected himself.

Cari was different than anyone else he'd ever known, and that couldn't be clearer than it was at this moment. He took one step toward her and she smiled at him, but he saw a hint of sadness in it. He was so afraid that he couldn't be the man she needed him to be.

It wasn't just that emotions were foreign to him, it was that he had no way to balance the one thing he'd always wanted—Montrose acceptance—with the one thing he just realized he couldn't survive without. Her love.

Love was ephemeral and always just out of his grasp. She might be looking at him right now with love in her eyes, but how long could that last? Would she still feel that way when her sisters were out of a job and her family's legacy was in ruins around her?

He doubted it. How could he be enough to keep her happy? How could he be the one thing that gave her hope when he knew he wasn't lovable and had never been enough for anyone else?

Cari woke up early as she usually did and rolled over to look at Dec as he lay sleeping next to her. He'd woken her once in the night to make love and she'd enjoyed it and having him here. She didn't get a chance to tell him how she felt about him because she could tell that he was struggling.

If she had to guess, she'd say he wasn't sure how to handle his own feelings. From everything she knew of his childhood, she knew that he hadn't grown up in a loving home, and part of her wanted to just make up for every second of that. But she knew she couldn't.

She leaned over and touched the stubble on his cheek

with one finger. He didn't look so tough and ready to take on the world sleeping like this. It reminded her of how tender his face had looked after he'd made love to her outside.

It was hard for her to reconcile, but there was vulnerability in Dec that she hadn't realized was there. She rolled over before she did something silly, like drawing hearts on his chest with her finger and then waking him up to make love again.

She wanted to see what he was like this morning; if the gamble she was taking with her heart was going to pay off or if she was going to end up broken and alone again.

She shook her head as she got out of bed, grabbed her robe and left the room. There was a big board meeting this morning at the Playtone Games office building, where Dec would be giving his results to her and her sisters as well as the executive committee from Playtone. She and her sisters had a mock-up demo of their IOS Christmas game ready to show them and were hoping to use that as leverage to keep the Infinity brand alive.

She checked on DJ, who was awake and playing with his stuffed animal in his crib. "Morning, little man."

"Mama," he said. She got him out of the crib, changed his diaper and dressed him for the day before going into the kitchen to feed him. She heard the shower come on in her bathroom and knew that Dec was up.

She told herself it was silly to be nervous, yet the longer she sat there waiting for him the more that feeling grew. She finished with DJ and took the baby and her mug of coffee down the hall to the master bedroom. DJ squirmed to get down and she set him on the floor to go into her closet and get her clothes for the day. She heard the door open to the bathroom.

"Dada," DJ said.

Cari came out of the closet and looked over at Dec. In this moment, they felt like a real family. Except as he looked at her, she realized he didn't look restless at all. And she felt the tinge of doubt in her heart. She loved him; surely he felt the same way about her.

Why would he have stayed last night if he didn't?

She had no answers, and for the first time she recognized that love made her vulnerable. She needed something from Dec that he might not be able to give her. And it wasn't fair of her to ask for it. Love wasn't the sunshiny emotion she'd hoped it would be. And given the way that her relationship with Dec had developed, why was that a surprise?

"Morning," he said, his voice gruff with sleep. "I used your razor to shave. I hope that's okay."

"Yes, of course it is. Um…are you coming to my office this morning or just going straight to Playtone?"

"I have to go home and change first," he said. "But then I'll just go to Playtone. Cari, today is going to be a long day."

She saw the weight of the coming day on his shoulders. She took a deep breath. "I know it's going to be hard on everyone. But I've been working on those financial targets that Allan set. I think you might be surprised by some of the things I have to show you today."

He gave her a vague half smile. "That will be good. Do you need anything from me for your presentation?"

"No," she said. "Why would I?"

He shook his head. "Kell is going to be a tough customer, honey. Whatever presentation you make, it had better be solid and have documentation to back it up."

"It will," she said. "Do you think it's going to be bad news?"

"There are going to be reductions," he said. "But I can't say any more than that."

She nodded and she felt a knot of fear in her stomach. It didn't sound good for Infinity, but she was realistic. From the beginning she had the feeling that she and her sisters had been on the chopping block. She could only hope the new game and revenue stream she'd found would be enough to give them some more time in their jobs.

"Don't worry about it. I know you are just doing your job."

"Do you need me to watch DJ while you shower?" he asked.

"Do you have the time?" she asked. "Normally I bring him in with me, but I got him dressed to save time."

"I'll watch him," Dec said.

She started toward the bathroom, but then stopped and looked over at Dec. "I wish we could make the world go away."

"Me, too. But I think we both knew from the beginning that was never going to happen. Everything between us is going to be influenced by your sisters, my cousins and the feud our grandfathers started."

"I know. I was just wishing life would be simpler. When the dust settles from the meeting today, we have to talk. I meant to discuss something with you last night, but I got distracted."

"By me?" he asked, coming over and wrapping his arms around her waist and pulling her back against him. "Want to be distracted again?"

"I'd love to, but I think I'm going to need to be on time in order to impress the Playtone board."

"Yes, you are. Just relax when you get in there and

let them see how much you care about the company. And show off your smarts."

"How do I do that?" she asked, glancing over her shoulder at him.

"By being yourself."

"I'll try."

"You'll do it. I know you will," he said, giving her a tender kiss before nudging her toward the bathroom.

She had her shower and Dec left when she did. She headed toward the Infinity Games offices and he went home to change. She couldn't help but feel that even though he'd stayed the night with her, he'd pulled back from her a little bit.

Dec didn't head to the Playtone Games office building after he'd been to his yacht and gotten dressed for the day. Instead he detoured out of his way and went to the Beverly Hills mansion he'd grown up in. As he fumbled in the glove box for the remote control to the large gate that surrounded the place, he sat there remembering the first day he'd arrived here.

He'd been four, so his memories were hazy. He only knew that he had a new family, but he hadn't been told that they were wealthy, so the big house had been a bit of a shock. The wrought-iron gates with the ornate *L* on them for his mother's maiden name, Lingle, had opened just as slowly then as they did today. And as he gunned the powerful Maserati engine and shot up the driveway, he realized that no matter what happened today, he wasn't going to change inside.

He had never felt like a Montrose, partly because of the adoption, but as he got out of his car and walked to the front door of the mansion, he realized the other reason was his mother.

He'd asked her once when he was sixteen and she'd been railing against his dad why she'd married him, and Helene had said that she'd been fooled by love.

He opened the front door of the mansion. It was quiet with just the whir of the air-conditioning, and it smelled of fresh lemons. Though it sat empty, he paid a staff to clean it once a week.

With his mother's words echoing in his head, he wandered through the big house where he'd grown up and realized that part of his fear was that Cari was playing him. There had been something almost desperate in her tone when she'd asked about the meeting later in the day. They both knew that Infinity Games was history and soon there would be little left from Gregory Chandler's original company.

But beyond that, was there more to the two of them than a son? What was this emotion that kept making him want to give up sound business logic and do what his gut insisted and save Cari's job? Was it love? He didn't know. His mother had been unable or unwilling to describe what love was. All that Dec could remember was that he never wanted to feel the way his mother had felt. She'd lost herself in drink to numb the way she felt when she'd realized his father had married her for her money.

What if everything Cari had done had been to get him to try to betray his cousins and save her and her sisters?

He rubbed the back of his neck and knew there were no answers here in the past. He had to make a decision today. He had to trust Cari and the new life that she seemed to want to build with him.

That future shouldn't frighten him as much as it did, but he didn't know how to build a life with her. Or anyone. He didn't feel content or safe with the thought of having Cari by his side because he knew how fragile his hold on her was. He had no idea how to stay. Six weeks was one thing, but a lifetime? Could he do it?

Would she even want him for that long? He hated not knowing. This, he realized, was the worst part of falling for Cari—he didn't know how she really felt about him. Was it just that she wanted him to be a father to his child?

She'd said she wanted to talk tonight. What did that mean? After the meeting, if he saved her, would she tell him of her true feelings or would she move on?

He shook his head. He wasn't going to change his mind or his plan for Infinity because of her. He'd just have to hope that she was smart enough to get that even though he wanted to make a life with her he couldn't do something that made no business sense.

He left the house and hoped he wasn't doomed to follow in his parents' footsteps. They hadn't planned on being miserable all their lives and yet neither of them had ever found any real happiness. He finally realized that he'd spent a lifetime running and moving so he'd never be in the situation he was currently caught in.

He loved Cari Chandler and he knew without a doubt that he was going to disappoint her today. He hoped that it would be the only time he did it, but he wasn't sure that it would be. His relationship skills stunk and he believed that her sisters would never approve of him in his life.

He knew the kind of pressure that put on a couple. He had grown up in a house where two families had been in conflict. As he drove to the Playtone Games campus, he thought that maybe old Thomas Montrose was having his last laugh on Dec. The son of the son that

Thomas thought would never measure up was going to be the man who gave him the one thing that the rest of the Montroses couldn't. The real revenge that Thomas had wanted—bringing a Chandler to her knees not just in the boardroom but in life.

And Dec knew this because he was going to sacrifice his own chance at future happiness to save Cari from him. He knew he wasn't the right man for her and this morning had given him time to recognize that he had changed, but not enough to be able to tell her that he loved her. And she deserved a man who could do that easily and tell her that every single day of her life.

Fourteen

Emma and Jessi were depending on her to wow the board of Playtone Games when the meeting started, but Cari was nervous as they waited in the empty conference room.

"Did Dec tell you what was in his report?" Emma asked.

"No. He'd never do that," Cari said to her sister. "He's very loyal to his cousins. Just like I am to you both."

"We get it. How serious is this thing between you both?" Jessi asked. "Patti said that Kell wasn't too happy with Dec that he was dating you."

"How does Patti know that?" Cari asked, feeling a little of her confidence dip. She hoped that Dec would have found a way to save all the jobs at Infinity, but she was realizing that was just a silly dream. No matter how much revenue she found with new opportunities, jobs were going to have to be cut.

"John's out here for a visit. He played volleyball with Dec and Kell and Allan and apparently there was some discussion that involved you."

Cari wondered if he'd told his cousins about DJ. She could think of no other reason for the argument. She knew that Allan had already known they were dating, thanks to that conversation in her conference room.

She didn't have time to say anything else to her sisters as the door opened and in walked Kell Montrose. The first thing that Cari noticed about him was that his eyes were icy and hard. He looked over at the three of them with such disdain she felt a chill move over her. And Cari knew that this wasn't going to go the way she'd hoped it would.

Allan came in next, looking pensive and serious, and then came Dec. He didn't look at her or her sisters, and she nervously shuffled her presentation in front of her on the conference table.

Jessi reached underneath the table to pat her thigh and she squeezed her sister's hand before she cleared her throat.

"Before we get started, I'd like to tell you about some changes to our financial revenue streams," Cari said. "Would you allow me to do that?"

"We weren't expecting this," Kell said. "I doubt anything you could say at this point would change our plans."

"This is a significant addition to our bottom line and exceeds the targets I discussed with your CFO six weeks ago," Cari said. She might be a pushover where her staff was concerned, but she could be as tough as nails when it came to fighting for them.

Kell turned to Allan. "Did you give her financial targets?"

"Yes. They are aggressive and she wanted to figure out how to save more of her head count."

"We didn't discuss this," Kell said.

Cari was glad she wasn't Allan, as Kell looked like he wasn't too pleased with his cousin. "No offense, Cari, but I didn't think you had a chance of meeting them. I'd like to hear how you are going to do this."

Cari nodded to Jessi, who passed out the presentation that she'd prepared with the financial numbers. She led them through the financial statement, which showed a clear 25 percent increase in profit margin with the addition of a new game.

"But this is all theoretical," Kell said.

"No, it's practical," Cari retorted. "I have a demo of the game on my iPad if you'd like to play it."

"A playable demo?" Dec asked. "When did you have time to develop it?"

"We used an existing game skeleton and changed the assets to Christmas. I used the staff who were scheduled to develop a new game for the second quarter next year, as we aren't sure if we'll need a game then. They have really worked hard on it."

She handed the iPad over to Kell and all three of the men took a turn playing the demo before handing it back to Cari.

"I'm impressed. This is the kind of innovative thinking we reward at Playtone," Kell said.

"I'm glad to hear it," Cari said.

"Make sure that Dec has a list of everyone who was involved in this project," Kell said.

Cari nodded, and Dec smiled over at her. She felt good about the presentation, and she hoped it was enough to make Kell see that there was merit to this generation of Chandlers.

"Should we reconvene in a few weeks?" Emma asked. "Now that you've seen what else we are capable of?"

Kell shook his head. "No, this changes nothing of our current plans. Dec, please begin your presentation."

Emma paled and Cari felt a sinking feeling in her stomach as Dec stood up. "I've had copies of my report made and they will be available to you three after the meeting."

"Why not now?" Jessi asked.

"I don't want you reading ahead and reacting until I've had a chance to explain. The new revenue stream will be added to my revised report, but as Kell just said it really doesn't change much of what we already had planned.

"When I first came to Infinity Games I noticed there was a lot of redundancy between what we do here at Playtone and what you do. For example, we don't need two technical development directors, so that is one role I recommend we cut."

Cari felt the anger simmer inside her as Dec went on and on, talking about all the areas he thought should be cut. She heard him say that three-quarters of the staff should be kept on as they were hard workers and possessed "cutting-edge design knowledge." At least some of her people were going to make the cut.

"Finally, I'm sure it comes as no surprise that I am recommending we cut the executive staff of Infinity Games," Dec intoned in an emotionless voice. "Though Cari, Jessi and Emma all seem to work long hours and are viable in their roles, there is simply no need to keep them all on. Initially I was going to recommend cutting all three but over the past six weeks I've seen how much the staff at Infinity depends on Cari. She's their cheerleader, motivator and they all work harder when she asks them to. I think she's an asset as long as we keep the Infinity staff on and recommend keeping her in an operations-officer role."

Jessi jumped up and started talking but Cari didn't really hear a thing that her sister said. Instead she only heard what Dec said. Was he recommending keeping her because of their relationship? She couldn't keep her job if Emma and Jessi were both fired.

She stood up, pointed to Dec and motioned for him to step to the corner of the room. Her sisters were having a very heated discussion with Kell and Allan, but Cari was interested in only one person.

"What was that about?" she hissed when they were standing aside from the table.

"What do you mean?"

"Why keep me and not Jessi or Emma? We're all vital to the longevity of Infinity Games."

"You are because you're in the trenches with your staff. But the other two—"

"Stop it, Dec. The 'other two' are my sisters. We can't build a life together when you fired my sisters."

"We're not building a life together," Dec said.

"What have we been doing, then?"

"Hell, I didn't mean it like that," he said. "I couldn't save all three of you, Cari. Kell isn't happy that I recommended you stay on staff, but I told him that was the only option that I would agree to."

"I appreciate that. But you have no idea the kind of situation you've put me in," she said.

"It was always going to be impossible. I can't turn my back on my family," he said after a long minute had passed.

"I'm not asking you to. I'm asking you to think of our son."

"I am thinking of him, so don't try to blackmail me with that. He's on my mind as much as he's on yours."

"Yes, but your side of the family comes out looking like the victors. Do you think we can be happy when my sisters are angry? I'm mad, too."

"Be realistic. It's a better outcome than you could have hoped for."

"No," she said. "I showed you how we could keep working as we have been. I showed you how Infinity Games needs to stay as it is. I showed you everything I had and it seems to mean nothing to you."

"Infinity Games is no longer yours to decide. You're lucky we're even thinking of keeping any of the staff."

She shook her head as anger and hurt coalesced inside of her. "Of course you'd say that. You don't know how to stick around and see the devastation you leave behind you."

"I'm not running away this time," he said.

"Well, you might as well be," Cari said.

"Stop acting like this. It's business, not the end of the world. You can't operate a business based on emotion."

"You can't because you're the Tin Man and you have no heart. But I'm not like you, Dec. I love you. But I bet that doesn't even matter to you. You don't understand how love changes everything. How it makes you aware of all the people around you and the consequences of your actions. You said this won't affect me or DJ but it will.

"I've been a fool thinking you could change. I believed you were someone who would stay and build a future with me and our son, but I see now you were never interested in that. And as much as I appreciate you keeping my job, if my sisters go, then so do I."

She turned to step away from him and became aware of the others staring over at them. She saw the faces of her sisters, who had no doubt heard her talk about her son's parentage. Their eyes were wide, their mouths agape. She took a deep breath and blurted, "Yes, you heard right. Dec and I have a son together. Even though he abandoned us, I welcomed him back into our lives thinking he was a changed man, though I see now he is still consumed with an old family feud that has nothing to do with the present."

"I knew it," Jessi said.

"You knew it? Why didn't you say something?" Allan asked her. "Seems like that's the kind of information you'd run with."

"I just got the report from my P.I. this morning. I should have said I suspected it." She turned to Kell. "You can't fire your own nephew's aunts."

"The baby changes nothing," Kell said.

"It changes everything," Emma interjected. "We're all related now and we can't keep trying to tear each other apart. It's time to settle the feud."

"No," Kell said. "I'm not giving up on anything because Dec and Cari had a one-night stand. That's not a commitment. That's a mistake."

Cari cringed at his remark. "Was it a mistake, Dec?" Cari asked him.

Dec glanced at her, and the look in his eyes reminded her of an animal caught in a trap. He turned his back to her and faced his cousin. "Kell, enough of this nonsense."

"It's not nonsense. It's good business sense," Kell said.

"Good business sense doesn't rely on revenge,"

Emma said, walking over to Cari and putting her arm around her.

As her sisters led her out of the conference room, Cari looked back at Dec. He looked stone-cold, as if he didn't feel anything. So different from the man whose arms she'd slept in last night. She felt her heart breaking into a thousand pieces and knew this moment was the worst of her life.

She started to cry as they walked down the corridors of Playtone Games to the elevator, and she couldn't stop. She felt Jessi patting her shoulder and she knew she should try to compose herself, but it was impossible.

She'd let herself be fooled by Declan Montrose again. It was bad enough when he'd physically abandoned her after their night together, but nothing was as bad as this emotional abandonment. After he'd spent weeks pretending to care for her, letting her believe that there was some hope for them… Well, it was just cruel, and it cut her so deep she didn't feel like she'd ever recover from it.

The sun was a shocking glare when they got to the parking lot, and she stopped walking, unable to go any farther. Her sisters wrapped their arms around her and held her close, and she cried in a way she hadn't since her parents had died.

She felt as if all of the hopes and dreams she'd had for the future were gone and she wondered how she was going to pick up the pieces of this break and move on. She wanted more for DJ than the life she now knew he was going to have. But she knew there was no way that a man like Dec could be the father she wanted for her son when he couldn't be the man she needed him to be as her partner and lover.

* * *

Dec stood shell-shocked by Cari's words. He shouldn't be shocked, he told himself. He knew she loved him. She would never have let him back into her bed if she didn't love him. That much had been obvious to him from the beginning.

But hearing her say that she thought he was heartless and that he was still stuck in the past hurt him deeply. He'd done his best to walk the fine line between what he owed his family and what he wanted for himself.

"You have a son?" Allan asked, walking over to Dec.

"Yes. I didn't know about DJ until I got back here and saw Cari again," Dec said.

"You should have said something to us," Kell said.

"Why?" Dec asked. "It wouldn't have changed anything."

"You're right. We couldn't change the path we were on, but I would never have asked you to manage the takeover," Kell said.

Dec looked at his cousin for a minute before he shook his head. "I don't agree with everything that Cari said, but she does have a point that we can't move forward when we are still consumed with the past. This was never about Granddad for me. You know he and I weren't that close," he said.

"Then what was it about?" Kell asked.

"I liked the challenge, and you two are family. We're all each other has left—or *had* left until I found out about my son."

"Do you feel like that as well, Allan?" Kell asked.

"I'm not in this for revenge," Allan replied. "I mean, sure, Granddad got a raw shake—"

Kell interrupted his response. "Maybe you both don't remember that Gregory Chandler deliberately cut Thomas out of the business for his own personal gain. That's not a 'raw shake.'"

Obviously, Kell wasn't going to be reasonable about this, Dec thought. And the argument was heating up to be the same one he'd heard before. Countless times. Dec realized he didn't want to rehash any of this with Kell. He stepped toward the conference room door. "My mother never really wanted to be a part of this and I understand why now. I don't know what's going to happen with me and Cari, but I do know I'm going to go after her. She's the first person in my life that I truly love." He stopped and banged his fist against the door frame. "Dammit, I told you before I've had a chance to tell her."

"Go after her," Allan said, gesturing to the door. Allan had a sort of envious look on his face. "Kell and I will figure out a way to make this more of an acquisition and less of a demolition of Infinity Games."

"Speak for yourself, Allan," Kell said, his anger palpable in the room. Kell was never going to want to make peace with the Chandlers.

As far as Dec was concerned, he had lost two things today—his son and Cari—because he no longer wanted to be a Montrose and live under the mantle of hate that they'd all been raised under. He understood his mother so much better right now than he ever had before this moment.

As he stood in the doorway, he saw Allan get to his feet and stride around the table toward Kell.

"We're not kids anymore, Kell," Allan said in a soft but commanding voice. "You're the CEO because we voted you into that position. But remember who owns the majority of shares." He leaned down to his cousin. "You either back down on this and let us find something that will make the future better for all of us or you might find yourself defending your job at the next meeting."

Kell cursed savagely under his breath, balled his hands into fists and pounded the conference room table. "I can't do this right now." Then he stalked out of the conference room.

Dec just looked at Allan. "Why are you backing me? We're not blood."

Allan came over and squeezed his shoulder. "We are blood. And we always have been. Once Kell calms down, he'll realize that your son is the future of both of our game companies. That it's more than making sure that Thomas gets one up on Gregory. After all, his grandson is a Montrose."

Allan had a point. But Dec didn't really care about all that. He could only think of Cari. He had thought he would be able to appease her after the meeting, but he'd heard the heartache in her voice and he knew that there was no way he was going to be able to win her back easily.

Allan stepped out of the conference room to go find Kell and try to calm him down, but all Dec could do was sink into a chair and think about how much he loved Cari. Business, money and the Montrose name meant nothing to him if he didn't have her by his side.

He picked up his cell phone and saw on the screen the picture Cari had taken of him and DJ. She'd given him so much more than he could ever thank her for, and she deserved more from him. Something that would show her that he really had changed.

But grand gestures weren't his thing. He might be the man to force a change, but to woo someone he had no idea how to begin. He hoped that confessing his love for her would be a start, but he had a few other ideas, as well.

It would take some time to put his plan in motion, but that was okay; he wanted to leave nothing to chance. Last night when he'd held her and come up with his plan to save her job, he realized he'd been too narrow in his thinking. He and Cari were part of something bigger, and he knew that he was going to have to get her sisters on board before he went after her and won her back.

Fifteen

"Sorry about breaking down," Cari said later that night when she was ensconced on Emma's living room sofa. DJ and Sam were playing quietly on the floor and she felt a little more normal now that she'd had a pint of Ben & Jerry's One Sweet Whirled.

"You were entitled to," Jessi said. "I would have socked Dec if he'd done that to me."

Cari half smiled, but she didn't think that was amusing. "I don't want to talk about Dec. We should be thinking of a plan to ensure they have to keep the three of us on staff. I'm sure that if I have the finance department rework our new figures—"

"We don't want to talk business now," Jessi said, interrupting her. "We all heard you say that you loved Dec. What are you going to do about that now?"

"I don't know," she said. "I really thought he'd handle everything differently. I thought… Well, I guess that doesn't matter. I can't make him into any man other than the one he is. And I get why the takeover and being a Montrose is so important to him."

"Yeah," Jessi said. "He's adopted."

"How do you know?"

"I had him investigated. I sort of guessed that he was DJ's father, too."

"How?" Cari asked.

"The investigator talked to the staff at the Atlanta hotel where you stayed and found out that Dec had been there, too. The timeline worked out to make him the dad."

Cari nodded. She should have known Jessi would figure it out. She was like a dog with a bone when she got on something.

"I suspected that Dec might be DJ's father when you started dating him," Emma added. "You'd been so careful to keep every man away." She put her empty ice-cream pint on the coffee table next to Cari's and Jessi's.

"I wasn't planning to say anything about DJ to him," Cari said. From the moment she'd decided to have the baby, she'd realized she had only herself to depend on. And then Dec reappeared.

"What happened? You never really said too much about it," Jessi asked.

"It was just a crazy attraction and we ended up in bed. The next morning he was gone, and I felt stupid so I didn't try to get in touch with him. I mean, at first I didn't realize he was a Montrose," Cari said.

"So when you realized you were pregnant?" Emma asked. Her sisters were both watching her intently.

"He had been out of the picture for so long and I didn't really want him back in it. It was so overwhelming, you know?"

"If I had found out I was pregnant I'd be freaking out," Jessi said.

"So would I," Emma said with a wink.

"You should have told us, Cari. I would have been the one to liaise with Dec if I'd known."

"You couldn't have protected me from this, Em. No matter what we did in the office, once I heard his name I knew I had to tell him about DJ."

"Why?" Jessi asked. "He forfeited his rights when he walked away."

"Because he's DJ's father," Cari said. "And you know we love our parents no matter what. Remember how Dad was always trying to please Grandfather and Grandfather never had anything nice to say?"

"I sure do," Jessi said. "Okay, I see your point, but I think you should have let me go back in there and pop him one. He was definitely being an ass today."

"He was on the spot. His cousins wanted him to gut all of us and he must have felt torn. I should have gone easier on him," Cari said.

"No, you shouldn't have," Emma said. "It doesn't matter where he was coming from. He owed you the respect of talking to you before he went in there with his proposal. They have to worry about their bottom line, so I'm not saying he should have done anything differently as far as cutting Jess and me, but he shouldn't have sprung it on you the way he did."

She wasn't surprised to hear Emma defending both her and Dec. Emma had always been fair-minded and she understood the way that business worked. They all did. "I guess I was just hurt, and the anger from Kell was scary. I don't want my son to be related to them. They are all so hard."

"I agree," Jessi said. "Allan isn't as bad as Kell, but you could see that they were definitely all united."

Cari sighed. "I'm kind of mad at Grandfather for doing what he did—cutting Thomas Montrose out of the business. I wonder why he did it."

"I don't think we'll ever know. But you'll certainly have a good story for DJ when he's older about why we don't like his dad's family."

That made Cari sad. She knew she'd let anger get the better of her today and she wished now that she hadn't. She should never have stayed on in her role once Dec came into the picture. She was never going to be blasé where he was concerned. "I should have stepped aside."

"It's too late now. We just have to move on," Emma said. "I think the staff would go with us if we started a new company."

Cari shook her head. She didn't want to be part of a new feud with the Montrose cousins. One where she and her sisters were starting on the losing end. She'd sacrificed too much to the feud already and she was done with that.

"You don't think they would?" Emma asked. "Dang, I thought they were more loyal."

"They might, but then Playtone would come after us again. I don't want to keep fighting the same battle," Cari said. She looked over at her son and decided it was time to go home. She wanted to hold on to DJ and pretend that she hadn't stripped emotionally bare in front of Dec and he hadn't just left her standing there naked.

"I'm tired, girls. I think I'm going to head home. We can meet tomorrow to figure out our next moves."

"Are you okay to drive?" Jessi asked. There was concern in her voice and Cari wondered if her sister realized that a broken heart hurt worse than any other pain.

Then she remembered that despite that outer toughness Jessi had a really soft heart.

"Yes," Cari said. "I'll be fine."

She scooped DJ up off the floor and said good-night to her nephew. Once she was in her car and driving toward her home, she realized she didn't want to go back there tonight. She didn't want to sleep in a bed that smelled of Dec or walk through her own house that was now filled with memories of him.

She drove to the Ritz Carlton and checked in there, and as she lay in the king-size hotel bed, she thought about the last time Dec had left her and how long it had taken her to get over him. This time felt so much worse.

She ran a bath and then climbed in with her son; he played in the water and she realized that his little world hadn't changed. She envied him the fact that no matter what had happened today or in the past he wouldn't remember it.

It took Dec and Allan all afternoon to get Kell to agree to give Jessi and Emma a chance to prove their worth to the company.

"I'm not going to accept mediocrity from them," Kell warned.

"I don't care as long as they have a chance to prove themselves," Dec said. "It's really all we can do at this point." He looked at his cousins and let out a breath. "I'm going to need a few days off to win Cari back."

"She said she loved you, dude, I don't think it'll be that hard," Allan said.

"She said she felt like a fool for loving me," Dec reminded him. "I should never have let her walk out."

Kell got up, walked over to him and clapped his hand

on his shoulder. "You will win her back. What can we do to help?"

"You no longer care that she's a Chandler?"

"You have a son, Dec, and as you pointed out earlier, that changes everything."

Dec was glad to hear it. Kell might be stubborn, but eventually he'd acquiesced to what was right. "I want DJ to feel like a real Montrose."

"What does that mean?" Allan asked.

"Just that I never really felt like one. I was always aware I was adopted."

"To us you were always a Montrose. I don't want to hear you say that again," Kell said.

He was glad to hear that from his cousins; he felt the acceptance he'd always searched for was finally his. Now he needed to get Cari back, and then he'd be able to relax. There was only one way to do it. He had to prove to her he had roots.

He thought of his big mansion in Beverly Hills standing empty and he knew what he wanted to do. "I have to trade in the Maserati. Will you two do me a favor?"

"Why do you have to trade it in?"

"It's not a kid car," he said. Then he explained what he needed his cousins to help him do, and they were more than happy to do their part. He had the feeling that Kell still felt bad about his outburst of temper earlier. Dec wasn't too sure if they would succeed in doing everything that he asked, but he left them to go put his part of the plan in motion.

He went to the Porsche dealer and traded the Maserati in on a Cayenne and then drove to Cari's house as the sun was setting. He was surprised to find it empty. He called Cari's number, but the phone just went to

voice mail. Damn. He didn't want to leave this rift between them any longer.

Now that he knew he loved her, he wanted his life
with her to start right now. He finally called Allan and
asked him to call John's wife and get Jessi's number.
Thirty minutes later he had it. It was after nine, which
was late, but not too late. Not when his future was at
stake. He called the number.

"This is Dec. Can I speak to Cari?" he asked when
Jessi answered the phone.

"She's not here. She went home, but I don't think
she's in the mood to see you," Jessi said.

"I'm at her house and she's not here," Dec said, feeling a sense of real panic. What if she'd had an accident?

"What? Are you sure she's not just hiding from you?"
Jessi asked.

"I'm positive. There is no one here and her car isn't in
the driveway," Dec explained. He looked at that empty
house and saw what he'd brought to her life. Maybe he
should just respect her wishes and let her stay hidden
from him. But he couldn't do that this time. The first
time he could walk away because he hadn't let himself care, but this time he loved her too much. And he
needed her back by his side.

"Let me see what I can find out," Jessi said after a
long minute. "If I help you with this, you are going to
owe me."

"Okay. I'll owe you a favor. But I can't do anything
to stop the takeover," he warned her.

"That's okay. I'll think of something you can do for
me. I'll call you back," she said.

"I'll be waiting."

Dec sat in the driveway of Cari's house for forty-five
minutes before his phone finally rang.

"Yes?"

"She's at a hotel. She said she couldn't face sleeping in the bed she shared with you," Jessi said.

Her words cut him like a knife. He'd never meant to hurt her like that. "Where is she?"

"Why do you want to know?"

"Why do you think?"

"I think you want her back. That you realized that you screwed up. But I want to hear you say it," Jessi said.

"I screwed up," he admitted. "Now tell me where she is."

"Ritz Carlton in Marina del Rey. She checked in two hours ago. So she must have gone there straight from Emma's house," Jessi said.

"Thanks," he said, disconnecting the call. She was staying less than a mile from the yacht club where he lived. He wondered if she'd done it deliberately. But he was glad she was so close. He knew it was too late tonight to go to her room, but in the morning when she woke up… He finally had the right gesture to show her how much she meant to him.

He drove to the hotel and talked to the concierge. They wouldn't give him Cari's room number but they did agree to deliver his invitation to her. He went to the yacht but couldn't sleep, so he spent the night vacillating between excitement at seeing her in the morning and the very real fear that she might not accept his invitation or his apology.

The envelope sitting in front of her suite door was white and embossed with the Ritz Carlton seal, but when Cari looked at the front of the envelope she recognized the handwriting as Dec's. She slowly opened it and drew out the card inside.

Please join me for breakfast on the *Big Spender* at slip number seven at the Marina del Rey Yacht Club this morning. I want a chance to apologize. Dec

It wasn't a wordy note, but she found she couldn't resist the chance to see him and hear what he wanted to say. To be honest, she'd had a miserable night and looked forward to a lifetime of lonely nights without Dec. If he wanted to apologize, then she wanted to hear it.

She got herself and DJ dressed after having the concierge send up outfits for them and drove over to the yacht club. She didn't need to ask directions to find Dec's yacht, as there was a trail of hearts with her name on them that led down the dock to the slip where she found the *Big Spender*. The gangplank was down and there were a trail of rose petals that led up to the deck, where they formed a huge heart.

"Hello?" she called out as she stepped on board.

"Hello," Dec said coming up the steps. He looked tired, as if he hadn't slept a wink the night before. He came over to her as soon as he saw her and took her into his arms. He kissed DJ on the head and then he kissed Cari on the lips.

"I love you," he said. The words hung in the air and he felt naked in front of her. For the first time he realized why Cari hadn't tried harder to contact him. She must have felt this fear when she thought of trying to get the man who'd fathered her son involved in her baby's life. The life of the child she loved so much.

She started to speak but he put his finger over her lips to keep her from saying anything. He couldn't let her tell him all the reasons why she didn't love him. He knew he'd screwed up yesterday and that it was going to take him forever to win her back. But he was okay with that.

"Yesterday morning when we left your place I knew it was going to be a difficult day. I also knew there was no way I could fire you and ask you to be my wife. And that's what I wanted, Cari. I don't know how things got so out of control."

"I think it was your cousin," Cari said. "He wants our blood. But it was also us. I wanted you to stop thinking like a businessman and just do what I wanted in my heart. And I made the meeting and the outcome into a big test."

"First, Kell did want your blood. But I said things to you I shouldn't have," he said. "You were right when you said that things are different now that we have a son. Everything changed for me the night you told me about DJ, and I was too afraid to admit it."

"I said things I shouldn't have, too. I was just so mad," she admitted.

She tipped her head to the side and stared up at him, and he saw tears in the corners of her eyes. "I love you, too. I want us to be a family, but I don't know how we can do that with the feud still going on."

"I agree," he said, cupping her face in his hands and using his thumbs to wipe away her tears. He hugged her close. "Business first so you can stop worrying about that. Kell, Allan and I have agreed to give your sisters a chance to prove they should keep their positions in the company. It's no guarantee for their jobs, but it's better than nothing. And Kell has agreed to be more civil from now on."

"That's a start," Cari said, wrapping her arms around his waist and resting her head on his chest. And finally he felt like there was a chance he might be able to really win her back.

"Did you mean it when you said you loved me?" she asked in a quiet voice.

"Yes, I did. I know you thought I didn't have a heart, and you're right. I don't have a heart because it belongs to you," he said.

"I love you, too, Dec. All those hearts that led the way to you…thank you for that," she said. "No one has ever done a big gesture like that for me. You make me feel special."

He leaned down and kissed her. "You are so special to me. I'm afraid to tell you how much you mean to me. I don't want you to have that kind of power over me, but no matter if I say the words or not, you still have it."

The tears were back in her eyes and she hugged him so fiercely that he felt the strength of her love.

"I want you to be my wife. I want to get married as soon as we can and start to live like a real family."

"I want that, too," she admitted. "It's the one thing I've wanted since we had dinner that first night you were back. I didn't want to believe that you could be the man of my dreams, but you are that and more."

"I hope I can live up to that, Cari," he said. "I'm going to make every effort to be that man. In fact, after we eat breakfast I have a surprise for you."

"Another one?"

"A few more," he said with a smile. He led the way to a table set up for breakfast for the three of them and when it was over he led them off the yacht to a Porsche

Cayenne—a family-style SUV that was the car of a man with a family, not a man who rode alone.

"This is my new car," he said, gesturing to the vehicle and the baby car seat in the rear bench. "I'm serious about sticking around and sharing my life with you."

She believed it. And she learned something else about the man she loved. When he made up his mind about something, he did it all the way. No half measures for Dec. He drove through the morning rush-hour traffic to Beverly Hills but wouldn't tell her where they were going. He stopped to send a text message, and they sat in the car holding hands while he waited to get a response. When it finally came he put the car in gear.

"Close your eyes," he said.

When she did as he'd asked, he turned the car down a residential street and a few minutes later he put the car in Park. "Don't open them yet."

She heard him get out of the car, come around to get DJ out of the backseat and then open her door.

He held her hand and helped her out of the car. "I've got DJ. You stay right here for a moment."

He left her standing in the midmorning sun; she thought she heard voices but couldn't identify them.

Dec was back by her side, alone, and he lifted her into his arms. He kissed her long and slow and when he lifted his head, he said, "Open your eyes."

She did, and saw a huge mansion with a banner tied to the front. For her and for all the world to see, it read: Cari, Please Help Me Fill This House with Love and Make It Our Home.

She hugged him close and buried her face in his neck, just breathing in the scent of this man she loved so very much.

"Yes, I will do that," she said.

"Good. I've already started by inviting our family over," he said.

Her eyes widened with surprise. She wasn't sure he'd really said what she thought she'd heard, but as he carried her over the threshold she saw that Kell, Allan, Emma, Sam and Jessi were all there, along with their son. Their families didn't look like bosom buddies, but they were all being civil.

DJ clapped his hands together. "Mama, Dada."

He crawled over to them as Dec put her on her feet. Cari bent down to pick up her son, knowing she'd gotten everything she could have wished for in love and life.

* * * * *

Look for the next BABY BUSINESS *novel,*
coming next summer!
Only from Katherine Garbera
and Harlequin Desire

#2251 STERN
The Westmorelands
Brenda Jackson

After his best friend's makeover, Stern Westmoreland suddenly wants her all for himself! Will he prove they can be much more than friends?

#2252 SOMETHING ABOUT THE BOSS...
Texas Cattleman's Club: The Missing Mogul
Yvonne Lindsay

Sophie suspects her new boss is involved in his business partner's disappearance, and she'll risk it all to uncover the truth...even if she has to seduce it out of him.

#2253 THE NANNY TRAP
Billionaires and Babies
Cat Schield

When his wife deserts their child, Blake hires the baby's surrogate mother as nanny—and desire unexpectedly ignites between them. But when the nanny reveals her secret, everything changes!

#2254 BRINGING HOME THE BACHELOR
The Bolton Brothers
Sarah M. Anderson

When the reformed "Wild" Bill Bolton finds himself as the prize at a charity bachelor auction, he has good girl Jenny thinking about taking a walk on the wild side!

#2255 CONVENIENTLY HIS PRINCESS
Married by Royal Decree
Olivia Gates

Aram's convenient bride turns out to be most inconvenient when he falls in love with her! But will Kanza believe in their love when the truth comes out?

#2256 A BUSINESS ENGAGEMENT
Duchess Diaries
Merline Lovelace

Sarah agreed to a fake engagement to save her sister, but the sexy business tycoon she's promised to—and the magic of Paris—make it all too real!

SPECIAL EXCERPT FROM

 HARLEQUIN®

Desire

A sneak peek at

STERN, *a Westmoreland novel*

by New York Times *and* USA TODAY *bestselling author*

Brenda Jackson

Available September 2013.
Only from Harlequin® Desire!

As far as Stern was concerned, his best friend had lost her ever-loving mind. But he didn't say that. Instead, he asked, "What's his name?"

"You don't need to know that. Do you tell me the name of every woman you want?"

"This is different."

"Really? In what way?"

He wasn't sure, but he just knew that it was. "For you to even ask me, that means you're not ready for the kind of relationship you're going after."

JoJo threw her head back and laughed. "Stern, I'll be thirty next year. I'm beginning to think that most of the men in town wonder if I'm really a girl."

He studied her. There had never been any doubt in his mind that she was a girl. She had long lashes and eyes so dark they were the color of midnight. She had gorgeous legs, long and endless. But he knew he was one of the few men who'd ever seen them.

"You hide what a nice body you have," he finally said. He suddenly sat up straight in the rocker. "I have an idea.

What you need is a makeover."

"A makeover?"

"Yes, and then you need to go where your guy hangs out. In a dress that shows your legs, in a style that shows off your hair." He reached over and took the cap off her head. Lustrous dark brown hair tumbled to her shoulders. He smiled. "See, I like it already."

And he did. He was tempted to run his hands through it to feel the silky texture.

He leaned back and took another sip of his beer, wondering where such a tempting thought had come from. This was JoJo, for heaven's sake. His best friend. He should not be thinking about how silky her hair was.

He should not be bothered by the thought of men checking out JoJo, of men calling her for a date.

Suddenly, he was thinking that maybe a makeover wasn't such a great idea after all.

Will Stern help JoJo win her dream man?

STERN

by New York Times *and* USA TODAY
bestselling author Brenda Jackson

Available September 2013
Only from Harlequin® Desire!